PIECING ME TOGETHER

Also by Renée Watson

What Momma Left Me
This Side of Home

PIECING ME TOGETHER

Renée Watson

BLOOMSBURY
NEW YORK LONDON OXFORD NEW DELHI SYDNEY

This book is a work of fiction. Any references to historical events, real people, or real locales are used
fictitiously. Other names, characters, places, and incidents are products of the author's imagination,
and any resemblance to actual events or locales or persons, living or dead, is entirely coincidental.

First published in the United States of America in February 2017
by Bloomsbury Children's Books
www.bloomsbury.com

Bloomsbury is a registered trademark of Bloomsbury Publishing Plc

For information about permission to reproduce selections from this book, write to
Permissions, Bloomsbury Children's Books, 1385 Broadway, New York, New York 10018
Bloomsbury books may be purchased for business or promotional use. For information on
bulk purchases please contact Macmillan Corporate and Premium Sales Department at
specialmarkets@macmillan.com

Library of Congress Cataloging-in-Publication Data
Names: Watson, Renée, author.
Title: Piecing me together/ by Renée Watson.
Description: New York : Bloomsbury, 2017.
Summary: Tired of being singled out at her mostly white private school as someone who needs support,
high school junior Jade would rather participate in the school's amazing Study Abroad program than join
Woman to Woman, a mentorship program for at-risk girls.
Identifiers: LCCN 2016023127 (print) • LCCN 2016049667 (e-book)
ISBN 978-1-68119-105-8 (hardcover) • ISBN 978-1-68119-106-5 (e-book)
Subjects: | CYAC: Mentoring—Fiction. | High schools—Fiction. | Schools—Fiction. | African
Americans—Fiction.
Classification: LCC PZ7.W32868 Pi 2017 (print) | LCC PZ7.W32868 (e-book) | DDC [Fic]—dc23
LC record available at https://lccn.loc.gov/2016023127

Book design by Colleen Andrews
Typeset by Newgen Knowledge Works (P) Ltd., Chennai, India
Printed and bound in the U.S.A. by Berryville Graphics Inc., Berryville, Virginia
8 10 9

All papers used by Bloomsbury Publishing, Inc., are natural, recyclable products
made from wood grown in well-managed forests. The manufacturing processes
conform to the environmental regulations of the country of origin.

For my nieces, Ashley Watson and Sydney Kelly

PIECING ME TOGETHER

1

español
Spanish language

I am learning to speak.
To give myself a way out. A way in.

2

tener éxito
to succeed

When I learned the Spanish word for *succeed*, I thought it was kind of ironic that the word *exit* is embedded in it. Like the universe was telling me that in order for me to make something of this life, I'd have to leave home, my neighborhood, my friends.

And maybe I've already started. For the past two years I've attended St. Francis High School on the other side of town, away from everything and everyone I love. Tomorrow is the first day of junior year, and you'd think it was my first day as a freshman, the way my stomach is turning. I don't think I'll ever get used to being at St. Francis while the rest of my friends are at Northside. I begged Mom to let me go to my neighborhood high school, but she just kept telling me, "Jade, honey, this is a good opportunity." One I couldn't pass up. It's the best private school in Portland, which means it's mostly white, which means it's expensive. I didn't want to get my hopes up. What was the point of applying if, once I got accepted, Mom wouldn't be able to afford for me to go?

But Mom had done her research. She knew St. Francis offered financial aid. So I applied, and once I got accepted, I received a full scholarship, so I kind of had to go.

So here I am, trying to pick out something to wear that doesn't look like I'm trying too hard to impress or that I don't care about how I look. St. Francis doesn't have uniforms, and even though everyone says it doesn't matter how you look on the outside, it does. Especially at St. Francis. I bought clothes with the money I made from working as a tutor at the rec center over the summer. I offered Mom some of the money I earned, to help with the bills or at least the groceries, but she wasn't having any of that. She told me to spend it on my school clothes and supplies. I saved some of it, though. Just in case.

Mom comes into my room without knocking, like always. "I won't be here tomorrow morning when you leave for school," she says. She seems sad about this, but I don't think it's a big deal. "You won't see much of me this week. I'm working extra hours."

Mom used to work as a housekeeper at Emanuel Hospital, but she got fired because she was caught stealing supplies. She sometimes brought home blankets and the small lotions that are given to patients. Snacks, too, like saltine crackers, juice boxes. Then one of her coworkers reported her. Now Mom works for her friend's mother, Ms. Louise, a rich old lady who can't do much for herself. Mom makes Ms. Louise breakfast, lunch, and dinner, gives her baths, and takes her to doctors' appointments. She cleans up the accidents Ms. Louise sometimes has when she can't make it to the bathroom. Ms. Louise's daughter comes at night, but sometimes she has a business trip to go on, so Mom stays.

I know Mom isn't here just to tell me her schedule for the week, because it's posted on the fridge. That's how we communicate. We write our schedules on the dry-erase board and use it to let each other know what we're up to. I close my closet, turn around, look at her, and wait. I know what's coming. Every year since I started at St. Francis, Mom comes to my room the night before school and starts to give me the Talk. Tonight she's taking a while to get to it, but I know it's coming. She asks questions she already knows the answers to—have I registered to take the SATs yet, and am I still going to tutor at the rec, now that school has started?—and then she says, "Jade, are you going to make some friends this year?"

Here it is. The Talk.

"Really, Mom?"

"Yes, really. You need some friends."

"I have Lee Lee."

"You need friends who go to St. Francis. You've been there for two years. How is it that you haven't made any new friends?"

"Well, at least I haven't made enemies," I say.

Mom sighs.

"I have friends there, Mom. They're just not my *best* friends. It's not like I go to school and sit all by myself in the cafeteria. I'm fine," I tell her.

"Are you sure?" Mom asks. "Because I swear, it's like if you and Lee Lee aren't joined together at the hip, you act like you can't survive."

Mom doesn't understand that I want to have Lee Lee to look at when something funny happens—something that's only funny to us. Our eyes have a way of finding each other no matter where we are in a room so we can give each other a look. A look that says, *Did you see that?* But at St. Francis, I don't have anyone to share that look with. Most things that seem ridiculous to me are normal there. Like when my humanities teacher asked, "Who are the invisible people in our community? Who are the people we, as a society, take for granted?"

Some girl in my class said her housekeeper.

It wasn't that I didn't think she took her housekeeper for granted; it was that I couldn't believe she had one. And then so many of my classmates nodded, like they could all relate. I actually looked across the room at the only other black girl in the class, and she was raising her hand, saying, "She took my answer," and so I knew we'd probably never make eye contact about anything. And I realized how different I am from everyone else at St. Francis. Not only because I'm black and almost everyone else is white, but because their mothers are the kind of people who hire housekeepers, and my mother is the kind of person who works as one.

Lee Lee would get that. She'd look at me, and we'd have a whole conversation with only our eyes. But now I have to wait till I get home from school to fill her in on the crazy things these rich people say and do.

Mom keeps on with her talk. "I really wish you'd make at least one friend—a close friend—this year at your school," she says. Then she says good night to me and walks into the hallway, where she turns and says, "Almost forgot to remind you—did you see my note on the fridge? You have a meeting with Mrs. Parker during lunch tomorrow."

"On the first day of school? About what?"

Mom shrugs. "She didn't give me details. Must be about the study abroad program," she says with a smile.

"You think so?" For the first time in—well, for the first time ever—I am excited to talk to Mrs. Parker. This is the year that teachers select students to volunteer in a foreign country and do service learning projects. That was the thing that made me want to attend St. Francis. Well, that and the scholarship. When we met with Mrs. Parker, my guidance counselor, I think she could tell I was not feeling going to school away from my friends. But she knew from my application essay that I wanted to take Spanish and that I wanted to travel, so she said, "Jade, St. Francis provides opportunities for our students to travel the world." She had me at that. Of course, she didn't tell me I'd have to wait until I was a junior.

Mrs. Parker always has some kind of opportunity to tell me about. Freshman year it was an essay writing class that happened after school. Sophomore year it was the free SAT prep class that met on Saturday mornings. *Saturday mornings.* She likes to take me downtown to the Arlene Schnitzer Hall whenever there's a speaker or poet in town, telling me I should hear so-and-so because kids in other cities in Oregon don't get these kinds of opportunities. I know Mrs. Parker is looking out for me—that she promised Mom she'd make sure I'd have a successful four years at St. Francis—but sometimes I wish I could say, *Oh, no, thank you, Mrs. Parker. I have enough opportunities. My life is full of opportunities. Give an opportunity to someone else.*

But girls like me, with coal skin and hula-hoop hips, whose mommas barely make enough money to keep food in the house, have to take opportunities every chance we get.

Before Mom walks away, she says, "I'm going to pick up some groceries after I get off work tomorrow. Anything you need me to get?"

"Did you see what I added to the list on the fridge?" I ask, smiling.

Mom laughs. "That was you? I thought maybe it was E.J. who wrote that."

E.J. is my mom's brother, but I have never called him Uncle E.J. He is twenty, so we are more like siblings. He started staying with us when he dropped out of college. Well, let him tell it: he took a leave of absence, but it's been a year and I haven't heard anything about his trying to go back. Instead he's busy making a name for himself as a local deejay.

Mom walks to her bedroom. "Mint chocolate chip ice cream. I'll see what I can do," she says. "If I have enough money, I'll get it. Promise."

I finish getting ready for school, thinking to myself that I know all about Mom's promises. She does her best to make them, but they are fragile and break easily.

3

dejar
to leave

The next morning I wake up before the sun. So early that only trucks and people up to no good are on the streets. There's nothing in the fridge but baking soda in the way back and half-empty bottles of ketchup, barbeque sauce, and mustard on the door. I drink a glass of water, take a shower, get dressed, and leave by six thirty so I can get to the bus.

I ride the 35 through the maze of houses that all look like one another, like sisters who are not twins but everyone thinks they are. Living here means when people ask, "Where do you live?" and you say, "The New Columbia," they say, "You mean the Villa?" and remind you that your neighborhood used to be public housing for World War II shipyard workers, and they remind you how by the eighties a lot of those apartments were run-down and how really, they were just the projects with a different name. At least that's what Mom says. She's always telling me, "I don't care if they give the 'hood a new name or not; it's still the 'hood."

Lots of people can't find beauty in my neighborhood, but I can. Ever since elementary school, I've been making beauty out of everyday things—candy wrappers, pages of a newspaper, receipts, rip-outs from magazines. I cut and tear, arrange and rearrange, and glue them down, morphing them into something no one else thought they could be. Like me. I'm ordinary too. The only thing fancy about me is my name: Jade. But I am not precious like the gem. There is nothing exquisite about my life. It's mine, though, so I'm going to make something out of it.

Not only for me but for my mom, too, because she is always saying, "Never thought I'd be here forever. But that's how things turned out." And when she says this, I know she means that if she hadn't had me when she was sixteen, she would have gone to college, would have maybe moved away from Portland, would have had fewer struggles. She never outright blames me for making her life harder than it needed to be; instead she pushes me. Hard. "Because no one pushed me," she says. One of us has to make it out of here, and I'm her only child, her only hope of remaking herself.

Dad saw a different future for himself too. But unlike Mom, I think I changed him in all the best ways. He's always telling me how I made him settle down, get himself together. "And just because me and your mom didn't work out, doesn't mean I don't love you," he tells me. He lives with his girlfriend, who I actually like, even though I'd never tell Mom that. Mom never talks bad about her, but I know I am not supposed to like this woman, who knew my dad had a girlfriend, a daughter, but flirted with him anyway. This woman, who is white and everything opposite of my mom, with her college degree and good-paying job. I try to stay out of any talk about Dad, his girlfriend, and what happened with him and Mom. At least he's in my life. A lot of my friends can't say that. Dad calls me his queen, says I am the best thing that happened to him.

I think about this as I ride to school. How I am someone's answered prayer but also someone's deferred dream. The bus moves and stops, moves and stops, making its way through North Portland. We pass the transition blocks, where North Portland becomes Northeast. Within just a block or two, you stop seeing modest apartment complexes and start seeing houses and luxury apartment buildings, restaurants with outdoor patios, and shops of all kinds.

The bus stops and four people get off. A white girl gets on and goes to sit in the first empty seat she sees. She has dark brown hair pulled back and twisted into a mess of a ponytail. She is thin, so it's easy for her to slide between the two people sitting at the front of the bus. She opens a book and disappears into it, never looking up.

We enter downtown and Book Girl is still on the bus. Anyone who stays on after this stop, besides me, is someone headed to work. She looks my age, so I doubt she's got a job to go to. I wonder if she's going to St. Francis.

I get off the bus at the same stop as Book Girl. She walks out the front door; I go out the back. I have never seen her before—and I would have noticed if she were taking the bus with me last year. Most of the students at St. Francis live over here, so they walk or drive to school. She is walking fast, too fast for me to catch up to, so I don't get to ask her if she's new. She blends into the flock of students entering the school.

There are a few sections of color in the crowd. There's Rose, one of the other black girls here, who I thought I'd become friends with because on my first day we talked about our braids and swapped ideas for styles. She's a year above me, so we don't have classes together and never have the same lunch period. But whenever we see each other in the hallway, we smile. I should have told Mom about her.

Then there's Josiah—the tech nerd who somehow in a place like this is one of the coolest, most popular guys in the school. I like him when he's with only me, when I'm tutoring him and drilling him on Spanish vocabulary. When it's us, he's regular, just a black guy who loves to geek out and experiment with making apps and learning coding. He's smart. Real smart. Just not so great at making his tongue roll an *r*. But when he gets around his white friends—especially the boys—he puts on a voice and uses slang and acts in ways that seem so opposite of who he really is.

Josiah stops me in the hallway. "Hey, a group of us are going to Zack's Burgers at lunch. You in?"

"Sorry, can't," I tell him. "I have a meeting with Mrs. Parker." He doesn't have to know I can't afford to eat out for lunch.

"Okay," Josiah says. "Next time." He walks away. For so many reasons, I want to say yes to him. Eating a burger at Zack's would be so much better than eating a turkey wrap from the cafeteria, but nothing would make me miss this meeting with Mrs. Parker. I can't wait to find out what country we're going to, what the service learning project will be. Of everything Mrs. Parker has signed me up for, this one means the most. This time it's not a program offering something I need, but it's about what I can *give*.

4

querer

to want

I am sitting in Mr. Flores's Spanish class, and I see that the girl from the bus is here too. Mr. Flores puts the class in pairs, and for a moment I think he's going to have the two of us get together, but instead I am partnered with Glamour Girl. Glamour Girl is one of the few black girls in my grade. But she doesn't exchange smiles with me in the hallway. Her real name is Kennedy, but I call her Glamour Girl because every time I see her, she is applying lip gloss or fixing her hair.

Right now her head is buried in her designer book bag. I look at all the things Glamour Girl is taking out of her bag and tossing onto the desk: a cell phone, a makeup carrier, a coin purse the same color as her bag, a small bottle of lotion, two kinds of lip gloss—one with a pink tint, the other clear—a debit card, and a small tin of peppermints.

I stare at the mints, and my stomach growls. Loud. I wish I could silence it. Big girls can't have growling stomachs.

Glamour Girl curses. She can't find her pen. I'm not surprised. I've never seen her with anything school-related. She puts everything back into her bag. Except the mints. She opens the tin and takes out one round candy. As soon as she puts it into her mouth, I smell peppermint and my stomach rumbles again.

"You want one?" Glamour Girl asks. But she is not talking to me. She is tapping the shoulder of the girl in front of her. Then everyone around us is reaching their greedy fingers into the tin, taking out small round candies. Someone passes the tin to me. There aren't any whole ones left. Just peppermint dust and a few that are broken in half. I take two halves and rest them on my tongue. I close my eyes and suck hard, savoring the cool flavor.

I give the almost empty tin to Glamour Girl and thank her. I am regretting that we aren't friends. Maybe if we were friends, she would have offered the mints to me first and I would have a perfectly round one.

When the lunch bell rings, I don't even stop at my locker. I go straight to Mrs. Parker's office, where she offers me candy from the jar on her desk. I take a cherry Jolly Rancher. Like most of the adults in this school, Mrs. Parker is white. I imagine her to be a fun grandmother to the three boys in the pictures that decorate her office.

There's a picture of her skating with them at Oaks Amusement Park. "Aren't they just the cutest little boys you've ever laid eyes on?" she says. "Okay, well, I'm biased, but still." The three boys have copper skin and tight dark-brown curls. I look at the rest of the framed photos in her room. There's a photo of a girl, who must be her daughter, standing with a brown man, the three little boys gathered around their legs, at the bottom of Multnomah Falls. Mrs. Parker picks up the photo. "My youngest and her husband," she tells me. Then she picks up a framed photo of her and her grandsons at a Winterhawks hockey game. They are all dressed in Winterhawks jerseys, and the logo in the center of their shirts is a Native American with four feathers in his hair and paint on his face. I wonder how a people's culture, a people's history, becomes a mascot. I wonder how this school counselor and her three grandsons can wear a stereotype on their shirts and hats and not care.

"Are you a Winterhawks fan?" Mrs. Parker asks.

"No, not really."

"Oh, too bad. I get free tickets all the time. Let me know if you ever want to check them out."

"Thank you," I say. Why do people who can afford anything they want get stuff for free all the time?

"Now let's get to business," Mrs. Parker says.

I take a deep breath and prepare to act surprised when she tells me she's nominating me for the study abroad program. She picks up a folder, looks at it, and like an orator who decides to improv instead of using her notes, tosses the folder back onto her desk and asks, "Jade, what do you want?"

To eat.

To travel with the study abroad program. Maybe go to Argentina.

To taste asado hot off the fire.

To lick my fingers after enjoying sweet alfajores—the dulce de leche dancing on my tongue.

To eat and speak Spanish in Argentina, in Costa Rica. In New York, California. In job interviews where knowing more than one language moves your application to the top of the pile.

To give myself a way out. A way in. Because language can take you places.

Mrs. Parker clears her throat. "It's okay if you don't have an answer yet," she says. "That's why I'm here. To help you figure it out. To help you get it once you know what *it* is." She picks the folder back up and hands it to me.

The front of the folder shows a group of black women—adults and teens—smiling and embracing one another. *Woman to Woman: A Mentorship Program for African American Girls.* Mrs. Parker is smiling like what she's about to tell me is that she found the cure for cancer. But really, what she has to tell me sounds more like a honking horn that's stuck, a favorite glass shattering into countless pieces on the floor.

Mrs. Parker tells me that twelve girls from high schools throughout the city have been selected to participate in Woman to Woman. Each of us will be paired with a mentor. "Look at all the great activities that are planned for you," she says. She takes the folder from my hand and opens it, pulling out a sheet titled *Monthly Outings*:

A Night at Oregon Symphony

Museum Visit at Portland Art Museum

Fun Day at Oaks Amusement Park

"Do you have any questions?" Mrs. Parker asks.

I want to speak up, ask, *What about the nomination for the study abroad program?* I want to ask about that day she looked into my eyes and said, *"St. Francis provides opportunities for our students to travel the world,"* but instead I ask, "Why was I chosen for this?"

Mrs. Parker clears her throat. "Well, uh, selection was based on, uh, gender, grade, and, well, several other things."

"Like?"

"Well, uh, several things. Teacher nominations . . . uh, need."

"Mrs. Parker, I don't need a mentor," I tell her.

"Every young person could use a caring adult in her life."

"I have my mother." And my uncle, and my dad. "You think I don't have anyone who cares about me?"

"No, no. That's not what I said." Mrs. Parker clears her throat. "We want to be as proactive as possible, and you know, well, statistics tell us that young people with your set of circumstances are, well, at risk for certain things, and we'd like to help you navigate through those circumstances." Mrs. Parker takes a candy out of her jar and pops it into her mouth. "I'd like you to thoroughly look over the information and consider it. This is a good *opportunity* for you."

That word shadows me. Follows me like a stray cat.

I stand up. "What happens if I don't participate?" I ask.

"If you *do* participate and complete the two-year program—keeping your grade point average at a three point five or above—you are awarded a scholarship to any Oregon college," Mrs. Parker tells me.

A scholarship to college?

I sit down, lean back in the seat, hear Mrs. Parker out.

She lowers her voice and talks as if what she is telling me is off the record. "You know, my son-in-law grew up in your same neighborhood. He lives in Lake Oswego now. Not a lot of African Americans live there, you know. And, well, he's a grown man, and even he's having a hard time adjusting. So, well, I think this school can be hard for anyone, but especially if you don't really have anyone who, you know, you can relate to. That's why I selected a mentor for you who went to this school," Mrs. Parker says. "She graduated four years ago. And now she's a graduate of Portland State University. You remind me so much of her," she says.

I don't say anything. I've already made up my mind that I'm going to do this, but I'm kind of enjoying listening to Mrs. Parker beg a little.

"Jade. You're a smart girl. Are you really going to pass on a chance to get a scholarship to college?"

"I'll do it," I say. And then: "Thank you for the *opportunity.*"

She hands me a sheet of paper with a list of questions on it. "We'll give this to your mentor before you meet so she can learn a little about you," she says. She hands me a pen.

I fill out the form.

Name: *Jade Butler*
Favorite Color: *Yellow*
Hobbies: *Collaging*

And then there's a question:

What do you hope to get out of this program?

I leave that one blank.

5

promesa
promise

Mom's scent hugs me as soon as I get in the door. She is stretched out on her twin bed. And even though she is resting, I can tell by her face that there is no peace for her, not even in her dreams.

She did not bother to take off her nylons or her shoes that she says are more comfortable than clouds. The TV is watching her, so I turn it off. Mom likes to go to sleep to noise. I think the voices keep her from feeling lonely.

In the kitchen, there are empty brown paper bags on the counter top, which means there are groceries. I open the door to the fridge: milk, butter, mayonnaise, bread, eggs, hot dogs. And in the pantry: peanut butter, jelly, cans of tuna, packages of Top Ramen. And in the freezer: family value–size ground beef, frozen pizzas. And in the way, way back—ice cream. Mint chocolate chip.

6

historia
history

Lee Lee comes over after school, and over bowls of mint choco-late chip ice cream, we swap stories about our first day. Before we can get good into our conversation, E.J. comes home, smelling up the whole living room with his cologne. He joins us at the kitchen table, but not before grabbing a spoon from the dish rack and helping himself to my bowl. I give him the meanest look I can muster.

"I mean, you can't share with your favorite uncle?" he says.

"Get your own." I point to the freezer and move my bowl closer to me.

He laughs, goes into the living room, and puts his headphones on and starts bobbing his head.

"Okay, what were you saying?" I ask Lee Lee.

She is laughing at the two of us and shaking her head. "I was just saying how much I like my history teacher. She's my favorite already," Lee Lee tells me.

"Why?" I ask.

"She's all about teaching stuff we don't necessarily learn in our textbooks. Like today we learned about York—the black slave who traveled with Lewis and Clark."

"A black person was part of the Lewis and Clark expedition? Really?"

Lee Lee tells me, "My teacher says he was just as important as Lewis and Clark." She reaches into her backpack and pulls out a work sheet and hands it to me. A picture of York is front and center. He looks strong and confident. He looks so regular, like he wasn't a slave, like he wasn't treated like less than anyone else. Lee Lee says, "My teacher told us that York and Sacagawea helped during the expedition. She said Sacagawea helped to translate and that she was very knowledgeable about the land and could tell which plants were edible and which ones could be used for medicine."

"What did York do?" I ask.

"Mrs. Phillips said he was a good hunter and he set up the tents and managed the sails. Once, he even saved Clark from drowning." Lee Lee scrapes the bowl and eats the last morsels of melted ice cream. "When they needed to decide on where to go next or how to handle a challenge, York got to vote. Sacagawea, too. The first time a black man and a woman were ever given that privilege."

Lee Lee tells me that Lewis and Clark came with gifts and

that it was a ritual to have a meeting ceremony. At that meeting, Lewis and Clark told the tribal leaders that their land was now the property of the United States, and that a man in the east was their new great father.

They did not tell them York was Clark's slave.

They did not tell them that their new great father owned slaves.

I give the work sheet back to Lee Lee. "I wonder if the native people saw it coming," I say. "Did they know that the meeting ceremony ritual was not so innocent, that it wasn't just an exchange of goods?"

Lee Lee looks at me. "I'm sure they didn't. How could they know this was the beginning of their displacement?"

"But York and Sacagawea—they knew?" I ask.

"I don't know," Lee Lee says. "But even if they did, what could they do about it?"

I have so many more questions, but Lee Lee is on to the next topic. She starts telling me about all the Northside drama— who's broken up, who's gotten back together. I know so many of them because we all went to middle school together.

The whole time Lee Lee is talking, I am thinking about York and Sacagawea, wondering how they must have felt having a form of freedom but no real power.

7

arte

art

Lee Lee has been gone for at least two hours. E.J. is in the living room, turning the sofa into his bed. I have on headphones so I can block out the TV show he's watching. One of those real-life murder mysteries. He has the volume up so loud, I am sure the neighbors can hear.

I am sitting at the kitchen table, which is really a folding card table someone gave us a year ago. It's not that sturdy or wide or long, but it is enough. Tonight it is holding scraps of paper, the 35 bus schedule, and old copies of the *St. John's Review*—our community newsletter.

I am ripping and cutting. Gluing and pasting. Rearranging reality, redefining, covering, disguising.

Tonight I am taking ugly and making beautiful.

I am still thinking about what Lee Lee told me about York. I'm thinking about the walks I've taken through North Portland and all the signs that mark the journey of Lewis and Clark. I've seen these signs my whole life. Lewis or Clark pointing into the distance, the other one standing with his gun. York is not there; neither is Sacagawea. Or the native people who were already there.

I think about Mrs. Parker. How she has a black son-in-law smiling at me from a frame. How proud she is of her free passes to Winterhawks games. How she wants me to have a mentor. How she's always ready to give me an opportunity, a gift. Like what she is telling me is she comes in peace.

8

algo en común
something in common

The Book Girl gets on the bus again. She sits in the same seat, reading the same book. I watch her as we ride to St. Francis. A man gets on the bus, his cell phone in his hand, and he is playing music for the entire bus, holding his phone up like it's an eighties boom box. And singing along. And he can't sing—not even a little bit.

It is too early for this.

The Book Girl looks around the bus, and our eyes meet. She smiles, the kind of uncomfortable smile people give one another in these kinds of situations. I smile back. The louder he sings, the bigger her eyes get. And then—even though there are plenty of empty seats—he stands right in front of her, as if to serenade her. She looks at me and with her eyes, asks, *Is this really happening?*

I motion for her to come sit next to me. I pick my bag up from the aisle seat and set it on my lap. She comes over, full of disbelief and laughter. "Thank you for rescuing me," she whispers. Once the man gets off the bus, we burst into laughter.

"I'm Jade," I tell her.

"Samantha," she says. "My friends call me Sam."

"How do you like St. Francis?"

She looks at me with suspicion.

"I go there too. We have the same Spanish class," I tell her.

"What? Oh God, I'm so sorry. I didn't realize—"

"It's okay."

"So you take the bus every morning?" Sam asks.

"*Every* morning," I tell her. "I live in North Portland."

"And I thought I lived far from St. Francis," Sam says. "I live close to Peninsula Park. Looks like we'll be bus buddies."

"Yeah."

As we ride to school together, I make sure to tell her the shortcuts to get around the crowded hallways. I let her know which teachers she should stay away from at all costs and which ones to get to know even if she doesn't have their classes.

Sam tucks her hair behind her right ear and clears her throat. "Any tips about lunch?" she asks.

"I eat in the cafeteria," I answer. I don't tell her that my meals are free and part of my scholarship package.

"I have to eat in the cafeteria too," Sam says. "I mean, well, I don't have to, but, well—"

She doesn't finish her sentence. She doesn't have to. "Meet me at the sandwich bar for lunch. We can eat together," I say.

"Okay. Thanks."

The bus stops and we get off.

Sam is full of more questions about St. Francis.

I am full of questions about her. I wonder what Sam is exiting from. She must be coming from something.

9

esperar
to wait

September has come and gone. My daily routine is riding the bus
in the morning and eating lunch with Sam. Depending on what
I have to do after school, we go home together too. But today I
can't because today is the day I meet my mentor. I have to take
a different bus after school to go to the first Woman to Woman
meeting. It's at a library in Northeast Portland. When the dismissal bell rings, I make my way to Sam's locker before I leave.

Sam is looking into a mirror, trying to fix her unfixable
hair. Her locker is full of pictures of her cat, Misty, who
she found in the rain. Owners definitely look like their pets.
Sam's thick hair sheds all over the place. Her eyes are big,
full, and piercing. Her mouth, thin and overshadowed by her
cheeks. She swoops her hair behind her ear. "Ready to meet
the woman who's going to change your life?"

I laugh.

We walk outside and stop at the corner.

"At least someone notices you need someone to talk to. It could be worse. You could be me. No one ever thinks I need anything," Sam says.

The light changes. She walks away so fast, I can't ask her what she means by that. Can't ask her what it is she needs.

When I get to the library, groups of women are huddled in circles, mingling and making small talk. The woman at the front desk checks me in and hands me a name tag. I print my name in green marker and stick the tag to the left side of my chest.

The woman scrolls her finger down the list. "Jade Butler? Let's see—your mentor hasn't arrived yet," she tells me. "I'm sure she'll be here soon. Her name is Maxine."

"Okay."

The woman hands me a folder. "This is all you need to know about Woman to Woman. It has our schedule for mentor-mentee outings, a handbook that goes over expectations, and lots of resources for you."

"Thank you."

"Help yourself to the refreshments," the woman says. She points to two long tables that have been pushed together to hold fruit and cheese trays, chips and dip, cookies, and drinks.

Before heading to the snack table, I walk to the back of the library and claim my seat. Two rows from the last. I put my jacket on the back of a folding chair and set the folder down. I walk over to the table and put five cookies in a napkin, looking around to make sure no one is watching. I fold the napkin and go back to my seat, where I slip the cookies into my backpack. I do this two more times, taking chips, grapes, strawberries, and more cookies, and sneak them into my bag. This is something I learned from Mom. Whenever we go out to eat, we usually have dinner at an all-you-can-eat place, like Izzy's or Old Country Buffet. Once we're full and ready to go, Mom takes foil out of her bag and discreetly wraps up food for us to take.

On my last trip to the table, I make a plate to eat for now. When I get back to my seat, a girl is sitting next to my chair. "Hi," she says. "I'm Jasmine."

"Jade," I tell her. I notice no one is sitting next to her. "Have you met your mentor?" I ask.

"She's not here yet," Jasmine tells me.

"Mine either." At least I'm not the only one.

A woman stands at the front of the room and calls everyone's attention. "Good afternoon, everyone. My name is Sabrina. I am so honored to kick off another cohort of mentors and mentees," she says. "I am the founder and executive director of Woman to Woman, and I started this program because I believe in the power of sisterhood. We girls are often overlooked as if our needs are not important. And, well, I got tired of complaining, and wanted to do something about it," Sabrina says. She has a small high-pitched voice. She's tall and thin and the darkest shade of black. Her hair is braided in tiny singles and pinned up in a bun.

As Sabrina is talking, a woman walks in quietly, closing the heavy door behind her so it doesn't make too much noise. She stops at the table to sign in and write her name on a name tag. She looks regal and carries herself in a way that makes me sit up in my seat. Our eyes meet and she smiles. The greeter at the table looks over my way too, and points. I can't tell if she's pointing at me or Jasmine. Once the woman gets closer, I see her name tag says, BRENDA. She whispers something to Jasmine and sits next to her.

Am I really going to be the loser girl whose mentor stood her up?

Sabrina continues her welcome speech. "There is an old adage that says, 'You can give a man a fish and feed him for a day. You can teach a man to fish and feed him for a lifetime.'" She pauses and lets the meaning sink in. "Well, I like what Pedro Noguera had to add. He says, 'Don't stop there.' He says, 'Help her to understand why the river is polluted so that she and her friends can organize to get the river clean and make it possible for the entire community to eat too,'" Sabrina says. She pauses again for a moment, and then a wide compassionate smile stretches across her face. "Young women, this is what this mentorship program is about. We will have fun, yes. But we will also discuss some of the distractions and barriers to success and hopefully gain strategies for overcoming them." Then she smiles. "But first, the fun." Sabrina asks everyone to stand. "Let's all make a big circle, please. Mentees, please stand next to your mentors."

I look around the room one more time and watch each pair join together, laughing and talking and getting to know one another. Maxine still isn't here. Some mentor.

Sabrina says, "First, we'll have everyone go around and say their names. But to add a little twist to it, say your name with a word that describes you and that begins with the letter of your first name." Sabrina steps forward. "Okay, I'll go first—Silly Sabrina," she announces.

Then the next person says, "Hilarious Hillary," and the woman next to her, "Bookworm Brenda."

I think of names for my mentor: Missing Maxine, Mediocre Maxine, Mean Maxine.

This is stupid.

I'm ready to go. I look back at the table—the greeter woman isn't there anymore. I take my jacket off the back of the chair I was saving, grab my backpack, and sneak out before anyone notices that no one came for me.

I walk to the bus stop, thinking about the fish and the river Sabrina was telling us about. I don't really want to learn about the polluted river. I want to move where the water is clean. And I don't want to play childish getting-to-know-you games. If I'm going to do this program, I want to get something out of it.

As I wait for the bus, some man with holes in his jacket and a bottle in his hand comes up to me and says, "You got a number, Jade?"

How does he know my name?

The man's eyes are looking at my breasts.

I look down. Great. I'm still wearing the stupid name tag. I pull it off, ball it up, and put it in my pocket.

"That's not your name anymore?" He steps closer to me. "That's fine. You don't want to be Jade no more? I'll call you whatever you want," he says. He leans in as if he's going to kiss me.

I step back. Tell him to stop. I walk away, leaving the drunk man yelling and cursing. There is no bus in sight, so I decide to walk a few blocks to the next stop.

By the time I get home, it is dark and raining. E.J. is already turning the sofa into his bed, and Mom is on her way to Ms. Louise's house. She's staying there for three nights while Ms. Louise's daughter is out of town. Mom looks at me with her knowing eyes. She can tell I'm upset. She always knows how I'm feeling, even when I don't know how to put it in words. She is good at reading minds, reading the room, at having a feeling that just won't go away.

Like the night E.J.'s best friend, Alan, was killed. Mom kept saying she had this feeling, a feeling that something bad was going to happen. She kept calling E.J.'s cell, but he didn't answer. I thought she was flipping out for no reason, but later that night we got the call that E.J. and his friends had been shot. E.J. was okay, barely grazed on his arm. Nate was wounded badly, and Alan died at the scene.

Nothing's been the same since then. I think Mom only hears what she wants to hear, sees what she wants to see when it comes to her baby brother. Mom knows E.J. is not fine. He's not working a full-time job, and that money he makes from deejaying and selling mixtapes isn't going to sustain him. Mom asks him all the time, "Are you looking for a job?" He says yes and she believes him. She asks him, "Are you okay, E.J.? What happened to you was traumatic. Maybe you should talk to someone." But E.J. says he is fine and Mom believes him. I wonder, how could she get that feeling that night and know her brother was in danger when he was miles away, and not know he's in danger when he's right in front of her face?

Mom looks me in my eyes. "What's wrong?" she asks. "How did it go?"

"She didn't show up," I tell her.

"What do you mean she didn't show up?" Mom grabs her umbrella from the bucket by the door.

I just stand there.

"Does anyone know your mentor didn't come?"

"No. I left."

"Well, Jade. You should have said something."

"Why?"

"Well, don't you care that she didn't show up? You need to let whoever is in charge know that—"

"I couldn't just interrupt the event, Mom. Plus, Sabrina will know when she checks the sign-in sheet. I don't need to say anything."

"You have to start speaking up for yourself. I don't know why you're so shy. You need to—"

"Mom, it's after seven already," I tell her. This is my way of reminding her that if she doesn't leave now, she will be late for work. It is my way of telling her I don't need a lecture right now.

She kisses me on my forehead. "Love you."

"Love you too."

"Think about what I said, please," Mom adds as she steps outside. She opens her umbrella and walks down the steps.

I go to my room and try to do my homework, but instead my mind keeps drifting off to what Mom said. The thing is, I don't think I'm shy. I just don't always know what to say or how to say it. I am like Mom in so many ways but not when it comes to things like this. She is full of words and bites her tongue for no one. I wish I could be that way.

10

presentar

to introduce

I am on the phone, talking to Lee Lee, telling her everything that did and didn't happen at the Woman to Woman welcome meeting. "A name game?" she asks. "Do they think you're in elementary school?"

"Right? That's how I felt," I tell her.

Lee Lee and I talk until her aunt tells her to get off the phone.

I hang up as E.J. comes out of the kitchen and into the living room to convert the sofa into his bed.

There is a knock at the door. I look out of the window and see a woman standing there. "E.J., I think someone is here for you."

"Is it Trina?" He spreads a blanket over the pulled-out sofa.

I take a closer look. This isn't Trina. And on a second look, I think maybe she's lost and needs directions. She's way too pretty to be here for E.J. Her hair is crinkled and wild, all over the place—but on purpose. She's somewhere in the middle of thick and big-boned. I want to look like that. Instead I'm just plump. I open the door. "Can I help you?" I ask.

"Hi," the woman says. "I'm here for Jade. My name is Maxine."

Maxine. My mentor.

"I'm Jade," I say.

I stand there, looking at her, wondering what she wants. Wondering how it is she can show up at my house in the middle of the night and not at the event earlier this evening. She must expect me to let her in, but there's no way I'm letting her see my house. Not with the sofa made up as E.J.'s bed.

Maxine steps forward. I don't move at all. "Nice to meet you, Jade," she says.

I cross my arms.

"I'm really sorry about today," she says. "A ton of stuff happened that was completely out of my control, and I couldn't make it." Her cell phone rings. She takes it out, pushes a button, and puts it back into her purse.

"It's okay," I tell her. It's not, but what else am I supposed to say?

"Can I, ah, do you mind if I come in?" she asks.

I guard the door. "My uncle's watching TV."

"Oh."

"But, um, well, hold on." I close the door, leaving her on the porch. "E.J., my mentor is here. Can you go to my room for a sec?"

He looks out the window. "She is *fiiiine*. She looks— Wait. I know her."

"You do not know her."

"How you gonna tell me who I know?" E.J. says. "I was just talking to my boy Jon about her today."

"E.J., will you please go to my room?"

He finally gets up. I pull the sheets off the sofa and toss them into his closet. I run to the bathroom and grab the can of air freshener and just about empty it, spraying the hallway and living room. E.J. starts coughing. "Is it that serious?" he yells.

I pick up his sneakers. "Yes. It is. Have you smelled these?" I throw his shoes into the closet too. And then I turn the lights out. I flick the lamp on instead, hoping the darkness will hide how sad the house is.

"You owe me," he says. He walks down the hallway.

I open the door. "Come in," I say. "Sorry to make you wait."

"I just wanted to meet you and give you this." She hands me a gift bag.

Is she trying to buy my forgiveness? I think about giving the gift back to her without even opening it, but then I stop being rude and remember how upset I was earlier today, how I wanted to meet her, and how now that I have what I want, I need to appreciate it.

I open the bag, taking the tissue paper out and neatly folding it before I dig in. It's so fancy, I don't want to mess it up. I look inside the bag. "Whoa, look at all this stuff!" I fan through the different colors of paper—some prints, some solid. Then I pull out the oil pastels and the sketchbook. "Thank you!"

"You're welcome," Maxine says. She lets out a sigh. We're probably thinking the same thing: all is forgiven.

"I thought you could add it to your collage materials. Hope it's useful," Maxine says.

"I love it."

"So tell me what kind of art you make," Maxine says.

"Well, I like to take things that people don't usually find beautiful and make them beautiful. Like, blocks here in the Villa, or sometimes people in my neighborhood. I don't know. I get ideas from everywhere."

"Can I see some of your artwork?"

I walk over to my bookshelf, take my sketchbook, and hand it to her. "These are only small collages. I like to make bigger ones, on canvas. But sometimes, when there's no space, I just make stuff in this," I tell her.

Maxine looks through my book. "Wow, Jade. You're, like, a real artist. I mean—this isn't kid art. You are for real." She flips through the book and stops at the page of Lee Lee. Part of the collage is old photos from when we were in elementary school. In the image, Lee Lee is standing, her hands on her hips, wearing that serious look she always has. The one that says, *I can handle anything. Nothing's going to stop me.* I made the collage the day after her grandmother was buried. I took different scraps of fabric from her grandmother's old handkerchiefs and ripped up an extra copy I had of the funeral program to make the background. "This is really, really lovely, Jade."

"Thank you."

"I have to tell my sister, Mia, about you. She's an artist and she owns a gallery on Jackson Avenue. You two have to meet." Maxine's cell phone rings again, and she ignores it. Then, seconds later, it rings once more. She takes her phone out and looks at the screen to see who's calling.

"You can answer it," I say. "Must be important."

"Sorry. Give me a minute." Maxine answers her phone. "Jon?" she says.

So E.J. was right?

She pauses for a long time, and even though I can't hear what's being said, I know it isn't good. I can tell by her eyes. "I can't talk about this right now, okay? I'm at my mentee's house."

Mentee. I don't like that word. I just want to be Jade.

I try to act like I'm not listening, which is hard to do because the living room is small. I put everything back into the gift bag, even the tissue paper, and put it on my bookshelf. The whole time I'm thinking how I pictured Maxine would be a woman with strict eyes and a voice that says she doesn't play around. But instead Maxine's eyes look nervous and gentle. Like she's new to this.

But her voice.

Her voice is not mean, but it is rich. Sounds like those St. Francis girls. The way she hangs up the phone from Jon and asks, "Mind if I sit *here*?" like she has a problem sitting on the sofa, like she wishes there was something else to sit on. I mean, yes, it's low. So low you have to rock yourself a few times to build momentum to get up, but it's not dirty.

Her voice.

The way she says, "How precious is that?" when she looks at my bookshelf.

My books are stacked by height and turned so that the titles can easily be seen. I pull a book off the shelf and hand it to her. "I've had some of these books since I was in fourth grade," I tell her.

Maxine strains to get up from the sofa, and walks over to take a closer look at my bookshelf. There are plaques on the top shelf. Some small, some big. All of them have my name front and center. "Wow. You've got a lot of trophies," she says. "You are quite the scholar. That's great."

I smile.

We talk for a while about which teachers are still at St. Francis and how things have changed. I ask Maxine if she liked St. Francis. She says, "I loved it. High school was a great experience for me. Enjoy it. It goes by fast." We talk more about her experience at St. Francis, how she was the senior class president and how she was on the debate team.

"Were you a student in Woman to Woman?" I ask.

"No," Maxine says.

So she's never been at risk for anything?

"But when Mrs. Parker called me, I really wanted to be part

of it. It's my way of giving back, I guess," Maxine says. She takes her phone out of her pocket, looks at a text message on the screen, and puts it away. "Mrs. Parker always looked out for me. She was the one who convinced me to go to Guatemala."

"You've been to Guatemala?"

"And Ghana," she says. "I was in the study abroad program at St. Francis. You're a junior, right? Isn't this the year students get nominated?"

"Yes, but—well, I don't know when that's happening," I tell her. "They haven't announced the nominations or where the trip is yet. I want to go." I don't tell her how I went to Mrs. Parker's office, thinking she had good news for me, but instead it was about Woman to Woman, about her. Turns out nominations don't happen till after winter break, so I still have a chance.

"You really should do it," Maxine tells me. "Traveling changes you. It opens you up in ways you'd never imagine, and it makes you appreciate home."

"Really?" I ask. "Seems like the more you travel, the more you'd want to leave Oregon. Other places sound so—I don't know, so much bigger, more diverse, more everything."

"I think everyone dreams of leaving home, but trust me, the cliché is true: I've been a lot of places and there really is no place like home."

Part of me thinks it's easy for Maxine to say this because home for her has probably never been a tiny two-bedroom house with a leaking roof.

E.J. comes into the living room. "Max, I thought that was you!"

"E.J.!" I throw a pillow at him.

"Just came to get something to drink. Calm down." E.J. walks into the kitchen.

"Hey, E.J.," Maxine says. "How've you been?"

My mentor knows my uncle? I'm not sure how to feel about this.

"I'm good, I'm good," E.J. says. "You know, still working on my music. Trying to finish this demo with Jon." E.J. comes back into the living room, a can of soda in his hand. "Speaking of Jon—"

"Let's not," Maxine says.

"He told me what went down today, but you two are going to get back together. You always do," E.J. says. He cracks the can open.

"I don't know about that," Maxine says.

I wonder what went down today and if it went down while Maxine was supposed to be with me. Did she stand me up because of some drama with her boyfriend?

E.J. gives Maxine a hug. "Well, it's good to see you. Hope it works out." He looks at me. "Sorry to interrupt."

"It's okay." Maxine yawns long. "I need to get out of here anyway." She stands and walks to the door. "It's nice meeting you, Jade. I'm looking forward to getting to know you."

"Nice meeting you too. Thanks for the gift. I can't wait to make something."

As soon as I close the door, I go to my room and say to E.J., "Tell me about Maxine."

He gets up and walks back into the living room.

"Didn't you just meet her? Why you asking me?" He turns the TV back on to his murder mystery.

I grab the control and turn the volume down. "E.J.— "

"What do you want to know?"

"Everything."

"I don't know her like that. I mean, I only know her because she's on and off with my boy Jon. Sometimes she comes to a show I'm deejaying, or when I go over to Jon's to make beats, she's there. But they broke up today, so I doubt I'll be seeing her anymore."

"They broke up today?"

"I'm trying to watch TV, Jade." He takes the control from me and turns the volume back up.

I know the kinds of guys E.J. hangs out with. They're the kind Dad tells me to avoid. The kind E.J. says, "Just because I hang out with them, doesn't mean I do what they do."

I'm regretting saying yes to this mentorship program. So far my mentor has stood me up because of some drama with her boyfriend and shown up in the middle of the night with gifts like that's supposed to make it all better. All of this has me wondering, what have I gotten myself into? Has me wondering, what is this woman really going to teach me?

11

buenos días

good morning

The radio blares out today's forecast. Rain. I'm in the kitchen, pouring milk into my bowl of cereal. Mom reaches for the carton and pours a splash into her coffee. "So, I see your mentor came bearing gifts. That was nice of her."

"She chose the best stuff, Mom. Like, the good stuff."

"I see that," Mom says. She looks at the dry-erase board on the fridge and studies the calendar. On Monday I'm staying after school for a National Honor Society meeting. Wednesday and Thursday I tutor Josiah, and Friday night there's a one-on-one mentoring outing with Maxine. "Busy week, huh?"

"Always," I say.

"It'll be worth it," Mom tells me. She drinks more of her coffee, traces the rim of the mug with her finger. "So, when do

I get to meet this mentor of yours? I don't like you coming and going with some stranger I don't know."

"I don't know. Maybe on Friday when she comes to pick me up." I finish my last bites, drink my milk, and get up from the table.

"What's her name again?"

"Maxine."

"I need her number."

I pick up the dry-erase marker and write Maxine's number on the board. Mom always questions me when I meet someone new. In middle school she hardly let me spend the night at any friends' houses, even if she'd met their parents. She'd say, "I don't know what those people do in their homes."

Mom gets up from the table and washes her plate. I go into the fridge and give her the lunch she packed. "Have a good day," we both say at the same time. When Mom leaves, the door slips out of her hand and slams. E.J. doesn't budge. He could sleep through an earthquake.

I finish getting ready for school and head out to the bus stop. As I wait for the bus, a woman walks up to me, looking confused. She is holding the hand of a young boy who is almost as tall as she is. When she says, "Excuse me, excuse me," I recognize an accent. She points to the sign and mimes a question. I don't understand what she's trying to say.

"¿Hablas español?" I ask.

"Sí, sí," she says. She hands me a wrinkled flyer and asks me for directions in Spanish. She's at the wrong bus stop.

I point toward the corner and tell her which way to go. "Doble a la derecha—turn right." She thanks me several times.

When I get on the bus, I think about how proud Mr. Flores would be. He's always telling us that having a real conversation is the best way to learn a foreign language. I think about all the travel words and phrases Mr. Flores has taught us, how ready I am to use them.

¿Qué hora es? What time is it?

¿Dónde está la partida? Where is the departure?

¿Dónde está la salida? Where is the exit?

¿Cuánto cuesta? How much does it cost?

¿Tiene un mapa que indique las paradas? Do you have a map showing the stops?

I know Mr. Flores thinks he's preparing us for surviving travel abroad, but these are questions my purpose is asking. I am finding a way to know these answers right here, right now.

12

amiga

female friend

The day drags on and on. Once the dismissal bell rings, Sam and I do our usual stop at Mrs. Parker's office for our candy fix before we head home. Today I'm going over Sam's house. Mom was so happy that I actually wanted to hang out with someone from St. Francis, she barely asked any questions.

As soon as we get off the bus, Sam starts giving me disclaimers and warnings. "Okay, so my house is small and kind of cluttered because my grandparents refuse to throw anything away," she says.

She lives with her grandparents? I don't ask why. There's never a good reason for a mother not to live with her daughter.

"Oh, and I didn't clean my room last night. Don't judge me." We walk past Peninsula Park. In the summer, the rose gardens are in full bloom and the fountain runs, so people stop and make penny wishes. But now, since it's fall, the park is barren and looks lonely. Sam is walking so fast, I can barely keep up. "And if my grandma doesn't talk to you, don't take it personal. My grandpa says she has Alzheimer's and that it makes her moody and —forgetful, but sometimes I think she's just mean and old and chooses what to remember and who to be nice to."

We wait at the corner for the cars to pass.

"My grandparents have lots of health problems, so the food in our house is pretty bland," Sam tells me. "Do you want to stop at the store? There won't be much to snack on. Only nasty diabetic candy and salt-free, butterless popcorn."

"I'm fine," I say. I was hoping to eat something at Sam's because I doubt there will be much to eat for dinner when I get home.

"You sure?"

I nod.

We make a left at the next corner and keep walking. Now that we're two blocks from the main street, the houses are getting smaller and the yards aren't as groomed.

"Well, this is it," Sam tells me. She walks up the steps of a tan house and unlocks the door. Before stepping in, she yells, "Grandma, it's me, Sam. I'm home. I have a friend with me."

"Huh?"

"It's me, Sam. I'm home. I have a friend with me." Sam steps in and motions for me to follow her. She whispers, "We have to announce ourselves so she doesn't think someone is breaking in. She gets freaked out easily."

I walk behind Sam.

"You can call her Grandma or Mrs. Franklin," Sam whispers.

"Hello, Mrs. Franklin," I say.

She is sitting in a worn dark-brown recliner, watching the news. She doesn't look away from the TV.

"Grandma, my friend said hello. Her name is Jade."

"Huh?"

"Hello, Mrs. Franklin," I say again. Louder this time.

Nothing.

Sam shakes her head and calls out, "Grandpa, are you here?"

"In the kitchen!"

"Come on," Sam says.

I follow her into the kitchen.

Mr. Franklin is standing at the stove, breaking spaghetti over a pot and dumping the noodles into boiling water. He has an apron on. I've never seen someone actually wear an apron when they cook. "You must be Jade," he says to me. He wipes his hands on his apron and holds his right hand out to shake mine. "Sam told me you'd be coming over," he says.

Sam says, "Next time I'll go to her house."

Mr. Franklin asks, "Where do you live, Jade?"

"North Portland."

"Oh, so not too far from here," he says. "I haven't been out that way in a while. Used to have a friend who lived over there by the St. John's Bridge, near Cathedral Park."

Mrs. Franklin blurts out, "Nothing but hillbillies, blacks, and Mexicans over there!"

"Grandma!" Sam looks at me and mouths, *I'm so sorry.*

"Shootouts all the time. That's okay; let them all kill each other off."

"Grandma, you can't say things like that, God!" Sam yells. "And how is it that you can hear us now, but a minute ago—"

"Sam." Mr. Franklin turns away from the stove and puts his hand on Sam's shoulder. He looks at me. "We've lived here for, oh, about forty years, I think. Yes, forty," he tells me. "And our neighbors, the ones to our right, they've been here for, oh, maybe twenty years."

"They're black!" Mrs. Franklin shouts.

I try to imagine what it must feel like to live in one place for so long. I've lived in seven places—some houses, some apartments, never a place we owned. Mr. Franklin talks about all the new changes that have happened in Northeast Portland. "I know people say it isn't what it used to be," he says. "I've been here for it all. I suppose in twenty years, there will be something else coming this way, changing it all again. That's life," he says.

I don't know what to say to Mr. Franklin. I get it, that he's been here a long time. But I know people who had to move. Mom says it was because the taxes got too high or because they didn't own their homes in the first place. She says people who don't own their homes don't have any real power. I look around Sam's house. She's right: it's small and stuffed and old. But it belongs to them, so that's something. That's a whole lot.

"We're going to be in my room, studying, Grandpa," Sam says.

We walk through the kitchen to get to the back of the house.

"My room is this way." We turn left at the end of the hall and go into her bedroom. From what I've seen, this is the only room in the house that is proof a teenager lives here. The rest of the house looks like a museum of antiques.

Sam has a loft bed with a desk under it. Across from the bed are a small futon and a TV. "Sit wherever you want," she tells me. "And if you need the bathroom, it's right there." She points to a door, and I almost want to go in just to see what it looks like. Her own bathroom? I wish. Sam sits next to me. She takes her shoes off without untying them, and kicks them across the room.

I take my flash cards out of my bag. "Ready?"

"Wow, did you make those? I swear, artists make the simplest things look so good."

I laugh.

"These actually make me want to study," Sam says. She reaches for them and flips through them slowly. "Thanks for tutoring me. I need all the help I can get." Sam gives me back the flash cards.

I hold a card up, showing Sam the English side, and she says the word in Spanish. Then I switch and drill her with the Spanish side. "Now you do me," I say.

There's a knock at the door. "Sam, do you have a moment?" Mr. Franklin says.

Sam sighs. "Come in."

Her grandfather steps into the room, cuffs his cell phone, and says, "It's your mom." He steps out of the room but remains in the doorway.

I start going through my flash cards, mostly so I don't have to sit here and be awkward with Sam's grandfather, who is definitely listening to every word Sam is saying to her mom.

"School is school," Sam says. "I'm actually studying right now."

She is quiet for a while, and then I hear, "No, I haven't talked to him," and "Yes, I still have his number," then, "Well, I have to go. I have company and I'm being rude." She says good-bye and gives the phone back to her grandfather.

Mr. Franklin frowns. "That's all you have to say?"

Sam points to my flash cards. "We have a test on Friday. I have to study."

Mr. Franklin closes the door and walks away. I hear him say, "She's doing good. Of course she misses you, but she's a teen-ager. She doesn't know how to show it."

"Sorry about that," Sam says.

"It's okay," I say. "You know, you could have talked as long as you wanted."

"I didn't have much to say anyway," Sam tells me. "She'll call again, probably next month for my birthday."

"Next month?" I don't mean to sound so shocked, but who only talks to their mom once a month?

"Yeah, well, that's what happens when you tell your child you don't want to be a mom anymore and drop her off at her grand-parents' house."

Sam can tell I'm thinking awful things.

She says, "It's better for me here. My mom really can't handle being a mother." She tucks her feet under herself.

Instead of studying, we talk about our fathers: hers lives in Eugene and is married, with a son. We talk about Sam's older brother, how he's in the army and how she misses him and prays for him every night. We talk about how I don't have any siblings but have always wanted one.

Sam's cat is at the door, begging to come in. She opens the door. "Come in, Misty. Come on." Sam picks Misty up, running her fingers through her body of black fur. "So, tell me, how do you survive at St. Francis?" Misty fidgets in Sam's arms, so Sam lets her down. "Everyone is so—I don't know, not stuck-up. People are actually mostly nice there, but there's this, this . . . I don't know. I mean, my other school barely had any electives. St. Francis has a cooking class, a computer game design class, and a club for ballroom dancing. It's kind of, I don't know, weird. I'm not used to—"

"Having so many options?" I ask.

"Yeah. I was telling my brother how I could have taken Chinese or German but that I decided to stick with Spanish, and he couldn't believe it." Sam plays with her hair, gathering it all to one side and stroking it, then twisting it up in a sloppy bun. It falls out immediately, and she does it again. She tells me how her brother had it so much worse than she did because he had to be the parent. "When I tell him about school—or even how our grandpa and grandma took me in, he sounds—I don't know. Happy for me but also, sad. Maybe jealous."

Misty purrs and stretches her body. She looks at me but doesn't come close, stares for a long time, yawns, and then walks away.

Sam keeps talking, yawning, too. "My brother was just so-so in school. I don't even think my mom knew about St. Francis, but even if she did, he probably wouldn't have gotten in," she tells me. "Not that he's not smart." Sam can't stop messing with her hair. "It's so funny, because sometimes you wouldn't even think we came from the same family. I don't know how it is that my life is so different from his." Sam stops talking, stops playing with her hair. "Sometimes I feel bad, you know?" Sam sighs. "Sorry, I'm rambling. I'm not making any sense."

"Yes, you are. I get it. I mean, not exactly, but I know what it's like to feel kind of guilty for being the one to get what others don't have access to." I am thinking about Lee Lee when I say this. "When I first started going to St. Francis, my friends would ask me to tell them what St. Francis was like. I told them about all the sports teams we have. They couldn't believe we have a swim and lacrosse team, golf, volleyball, and soccer teams, track and field. They looked like they were in awe. But sometimes there was sadness in their eyes," I tell Sam. "There's also this pride they have, so I kind of feel like I can't let them down. And sometimes it's just all too much. So, yeah, I get feeling bad."

Sam leans forward. "But then again I feel bad for feeling bad, if that makes any sense," she says. "It's kind of not fair for us to feel guilty for getting what we deserve. We work hard."

It takes a minute for Sam's words to sink in.

I have never thought about my deserving the good things that have happened in my life. Maybe because I know so many people who work hard but still don't get the things they deserve, sometimes not even the things they need.

Sam picks the flash cards up and skims through them. "It's weird, huh?"

"What?"

"Being stuck in the middle. Like, sometimes I hold back at school, you know? Like I don't ever join in on those what-are-you-doing-this-weekend? conversations, because I know nothing I will say can compare to the weekend excursions those girls at St. Francis go on," Sam says. "But I also don't talk much about what I do at school with my family or with my friends who don't go to St. Francis."

Misty goes to the door and scratches it. Sam gets up and opens the door to let her out. "God, Jade. I don't know how you've done this for two years," she says.

"I don't either, but now that I have you, maybe these next two years won't be so bad."

13

hija
daughter

Woman to Woman has one monthly meeting where we all gather together, and in between those meetings we have one-on-one outings with our mentors. Last Friday, Maxine was supposed to take me out for dinner, but at the last minute she canceled. "Something came up," she said. And I couldn't help but wonder if that something was Jon. But today she's making it up, I guess. We're going out to celebrate my birthday.

Mom slugs her way into the kitchen, yawning her sleep away. "Morning," she says.

"Good morning." I hand Mom her favorite mug, the one Dad gave her a long time ago, one of those Valentine's Day mugs full of chocolates. No corny hearts on it, but it is red. All this time, she still has it. No one drinks from it but her. "I made coffee," I say.

"Thanks." Mom pours her morning wake-me-up. "You're dressed early for a Sunday," she says. "I didn't see anything on the calendar."

"Oh, it's a last-minute thing. Maxine called and asked if I wanted to do brunch with her to celebrate my birthday."

"*Do* brunch? You mean go to brunch?" Mom laughs. "How does one *do* brunch?" Mom pours milk into her mug, then opens a packet of sweetener and sprinkles it in. She stirs. "That woman has you talking like her already, huh?"

"Mom—"

"I haven't even met this girl, and she's taking you out?" Mom sips her coffee and then puts two slices of bread into the toaster.

"It's for my birthday," I say.

"Your birthday isn't until next weekend."

"She'll be out of town and wanted to celebrate before she left."

"Well, you still have chores to do. And I don't appreciate her not asking me. Tell her you can't go."

"What do you mean, I can't go?"

Mom looks at me, telling me with her eyes that she is not going to repeat herself. That I heard her the first time.

"But, Mom, she's on her way."

"You are not going."

"Why can't I go?"

"Jade, the answer is no. You. Are. Not. Going." Mom takes

butter out of the fridge, gets a knife and plate, and waits for her toast. Once the bread pops from the toaster, she slathers it with butter and eats, standing. "You can go ahead and get that sad look off your face. I'm not changing my mind."

The doorbell rings.

It's Maxine.

"I'll get it," Mom says. I wish she'd put on some decent clothes. At least take her scarf off. She opens the door, barely giving Maxine a chance to speak. "Good morning," she says. "You must be Maxine." Mom has her hand on her hip and won't let Maxine through the door. "I'm sorry you wasted your time and gas coming over here, but Jade is not going with you today."

"Oh, I'm sorry to hear that. I was hoping to do an early b-day celebration with her and spend some quality time together," Maxine says. "Is she okay?"

"Oh, she's fine," Mom says. "I would appreciate it if you contact me first before you and Jade make plans. Jade is not grown. Believe it or not, she does have a mother. That's me."

"I apologize, Ms. Butler," Maxine says. "I didn't mean to disrespect you. It's just, well, I know you're not home that often and so—"

"When I'm not at home, I'm working. And what does that have to do with anything?"

I wish Maxine would've apologized and left it at that.

Mom says, "Please let this be the first and last time you try to take my daughter out of my house without my knowing and giving permission."

"Yes, ma'am. Again, I apologize."

Mom moves away from the door and lets Maxine in. She walks into the kitchen. "Now, you're welcome to stay for a little while if you'd like. But she is not leaving this house. Jade has some cleaning to do." Mom looks at me, because she's already told me twice to clean my room and the kitchen. She takes her coffee and goes into her bedroom, mumbling the whole time about how I must think the kitchen is my art studio. "Got scraps of paper all over the place," she says. She mentions the paint I spilled last night while I was working, but I don't hear all of what she says because her voice has trailed off and is muffled behind the closed door.

Once Maxine knows my mom is in her room, she says, "I'm sorry, Jade. I didn't mean to get you in trouble or make your mom upset."

"No, I'm sorry. She's so—"

"Right," Maxine says. "She's right."

I cross my arms. "I really wanted to go," I tell Maxine.

"It's okay. We'll do a rain check. I'll be sure to speak with her about our plans," she says.

"Okay," I say. "You want to see the mess my mom was talking about?" I ask.

Maxine smiles, and I take her into my bedroom. In the center of the room is my scrap box. All around it are patterned and colored paper, maps, and cut-up fabric. In the corner, on my desk, is the half-finished piece I started about York and Lewis and Clark.

Maxine rubs her hands along the different textures. "This is beautiful," she says. "So many details." She stares at the piece, taking it all in. "I'm . . . I'm speechless. I mean, it's one thing to see your sketchbook, but this? This is—this is, wow."

Maxine stays for about an hour. We talk about art, music, and movies. And I have to admit, just like Maxine is surprised that a girl my age can create this kind of art, I am surprised a woman like her can relate to the movies and music I like. Every time I say something I love, Maxine says, "Me too," and I guess she sees the shock on my face because she says, "Why are you looking at me like that? You think because I went to St. Francis that I don't know black culture?" Maxine says, laughing.

I don't say no, but I don't say yes.

"I have good taste," Maxine says. "Plus, I'm not *that* much older than you."

Before Maxine leaves, she talks to Mom about taking me to a bookstore downtown. I hear her say, "I'd like to buy her a few art books if that's okay with you. Your daughter's got real talent."

"I know," Mom says. "She's very talented—and book smart, too." Mom always makes it clear that I can do more than draw. Whenever someone tells her how good I am at art, she reminds them that I'm good at science and math, too. Mom says I can go. She tells me to write it on the dry-erase board so she doesn't forget. "Nice to finally meet you, Maxine. I hope you know I wasn't trying to give you a hard time. I just care about my child. This is the only one I got," Mom says. "And at the end of the day, when this program is over, she's not going to be anyone's mentee, but she's still gonna be *my* daughter."

14

feliz cumpleaños
happy birthday

I wake up to the smell of pancakes and bacon. Mom is fixing my favorite breakfast. E.J. is at my door, banging like he's the police. "Come on, birthday girl. These pancakes are getting cold."

I get out of bed and open the door. "Morning."

"Happy birthday," E.J. says.

"Thanks."

When I walk into the kitchen, Mom is standing at the stove, working her magic. Strawberries are cut and already on the table in the bowl she uses only on special occasions. "There's my baby girl." Mom smiles at me and kisses me on my cheek. "Hope you're hungry." She adds more pancakes to a pile that is already on a plate. E.J. sets the table and we eat.

Mom asks, "So, what are your plans?"

"I'm supposed to go out to eat with Lee Lee and Sam."

"Oh, that's great, Jade. That's really great," Mom says.

"Told you I had friends," I tell her. I roll my eyes—just a little—then smile. "I keep telling Lee Lee about Sam, and Sam about Lee Lee, so they're finally going to meet today." I pour more syrup onto my pancakes. "And Dad said he was coming by tonight to drop off my gift," I tell her.

E.J. gives Mom a look. She puts a forkful of pancakes into her mouth.

"What?" I ask E.J.

"Your dad said he's coming, huh? Said he got you something?"

"E.J., don't start," Mom says.

"That sorry—"

"E.J." Mom stares him down. "Don't. Start."

"I'm just asking what is he going to buy you a present with? Wishes? Or is he going to use that white lady's money?"

"E.J.!" Mom is yelling now.

I get up from the table. "She's not *some* lady. She's his fiancée. And my dad isn't working right now because he got laid off— you never even had a job to get laid off from."

"He's using her, Jade. They've been engaged for, what, three years? That man is not marrying her. He is living off her."

"And what if he is? You're living off my mom!"

"Jade!" Now Mom is yelling at me.

I leave my half-eaten plate of pancakes on the table and go into my room. I don't come out until it's time for me to get ready to go meet up with Lee Lee and Sam. By then E.J. is gone and

Mom is off to Ms. Louise's house. As I am changing my clothes, the phone rings. It's Lee Lee. She can't go. She got into an argument with her aunt, and now she's on punishment. As soon as I hang up, the phone is ringing again. This time it's Sam telling me she is sick, so she can't come either.

I know I can't blame Lee Lee and Sam for not being able to celebrate my birthday. I mean, Lee Lee's aunt is always overreacting and fussing and putting Lee Lee on punishment for something. And Sam can't help that she's sick. But of all the days for them not to be able to hang out with me, why this one? I spend the rest of the afternoon watching TV and sleeping on and off.

E.J. comes home as the sky settles into its blackness. We don't speak to each other. He has a Safeway bag in his hand. He goes to the fridge and puts away whatever it is he bought.

Dad hasn't come, hasn't called.

Once it's eleven o'clock, I go into my room and dress for bed. I can feel the tears trying to come, trying to work their way out, but I distract myself by listening to music. I put my headphones on, find the playlist E.J. made for the end-of-summer BBQ at the rec center. Nothing but fast songs, some of them I don't even like that much, because they were overplayed during the summer, but I listen anyway. Because a fast song you kind of like is better than a slow song you love when you're trying to keep your heart from exploding. I turn the volume up and lie on my bed.

I'm almost asleep when E.J. starts banging on my door. I take out one earbud. "What?"

"Come here for a sec," he says.

I step into the hallway and follow E.J. He walks to the kitchen. On the table he's placed two slices of cheesecake. One has a candle in the middle. "Can't go to bed without some birthday dessert," he says. He pulls me into him. "We good?"

I nod and hug him back tight.

"You know I love you, right? You my favorite niece."

"I'm your only niece."

"Details, details," E.J. says.

15

el pelo
hair

No braids today.

My black cotton hovers over me like a cloud.

I'd never wear my hair like this to school, but today is Sunday and I'm home. When Mom comes back from work, she sees me and smiles. "You've been in my closet?" She tugs at the scarf tied around my head as a headband.

"You never wear this."

"Humph," she says. She takes her shoes off, sits on the sofa, and lets out a sigh. "I guess you can have it. Looks better on you, anyway."

I laugh and mumble under my breath, "I know."

16

regalo
gift

The weekend is over, and Monday has come with wind and rain. I hold my umbrella in front of me, like a warrior's shield, to keep the rain from hitting my face. I hold on tight to the top so it doesn't blow away.

When I get on the bus, my shoes squeak and slide as I walk to the back. Someone must have set their umbrella in the seat because it is wet. I find another seat. Sam isn't at her stop this morning, so the second half of the bus ride is quiet and slow. Like it used to be last year.

Once I get to school, I head to my locker. Josiah is walking toward me. "Hey, Jade. Happy birthday," he says.

"Thanks." I didn't even know he knew it was my birthday.

I turn the corner and walk past Mrs. Parker's office. When

she sees me, she walks to the door and says, "Hope you have a great birthday, Jade."

"Oh, it was Saturday. But thank you."

"Well, happy belated," she says.

I keep walking toward my locker. I see Sam standing at the end of the hallway. She is at my locker—only it doesn't look like my locker, because there are balloons and an oversize card taped on it. I walk faster, and when I get to her, she holds her arms out and hugs me. "I'm so sorry I missed your birthday lunch. I really wanted to go."

"Sam, this is so—wow, thank you."

"You're welcome," she says.

For the rest of the day, whenever I'm at my locker, someone calls out, "Happy birthday!" to me. Even people I don't even know. Having balloons taped to your locker brings a lot of attention. Usually I don't like attention put on me. But today it doesn't feel too bad.

17

mi padre
my father

After school I go over to Dad's. He can't keep secrets at all, so as soon as I walk through the door, he says, "I have something for you, but I haven't wrapped it yet, so don't go into my bedroom."

"Dad, I never go into your bedroom."

"It's something you've wanted for a long time. A really long time," he says. "I don't know why. You don't ever frame the photos you take. You just cut 'em up or change them."

"Well, no need to wrap it now," I say. I laugh when he looks at me, all confused, like he has no idea how I figured it out.

Dad goes into his bedroom and brings out two boxes. One has a digital camera in it, the other a mini photo printer.

"Thanks, Dad."

"Anything for my baby girl," he says. "I'm, uh, I'm sorry I couldn't see you on your actual birthday. Something came up."

"You could have called," I tell him.

"My cell died. I need to figure out what's wrong with the thing. Make one call and the battery is drained." Dad starts rubbing his head. "Don't give me that look," he says.

"What look?"

"Looking like your mother."

I conjure Mom—what would she say? "The point isn't your phone dying. Why did you need to cancel, anyway?"

Dad opens his mouth to give me his reasons but then closes it, sits back, and says, "No good reason, Jade. I'm sorry," he says. "I didn't mean to hurt my queen. I'm sorry." He walks to his room and comes back out. "I forgot about these." He hands me a new pack of batteries. I put them in the camera and start taking pictures right away. "Come on now, not of me," Dad says. "I didn't get you this thing so you could take pictures of me."

"One more," I tell him.

He doesn't smile, but at least he sits still.

As I take the photo, I am reminded that we have the same eyes.

"Okay," Dad says. "That was your one more. Now get out from behind the lens and come join me in here. He walks into the kitchen and takes out leftovers from the fridge. Three containers of Chinese food. He puts the rice, shrimp and broccoli, and egg roll on a plate and heats the food in the microwave. "How is school? What are you into these days? Besides art."

"School is okay, I guess. I love my Spanish class."

"What do you like about it?" Dad asks. He never lets the first answer be the only answer.

"It makes me feel like I'm learning a secret code or something. I don't know. It's powerful."

"Powerful? Really?"

"Yes, all language is. That's what you used to tell me."

Dad puts his fork down. Leans back in his chair. "Me? I told you that?"

"Yes, when I was little. When it was story time and I didn't want to stop playing to go read and you would tell me I ought to take every chance I get to open a book because it was once illegal to teach a black person how to read," I remind him.

"*I* told you that?" Dad asks, smiling.

"Dad, I'm serious. You told me that knowing how to read words and knowing when to speak them is the most valuable commodity a person can have. You don't remember saying that?"

"Yeah, sounds like something I'd say." Dad laughs. "Didn't realize you were really listening."

"Of course I was. And ever since then I've wanted to be a black girl who could read and write in many languages, because I know there was a time when that seemed impossible."

"So you're saying your passion is my fault."

"Yep."

"I wish I could take all the credit for you. But you know you get that big dreaming from your momma," he says. "Back when we were in school, she talked that same way. You just like her."

18

fotografiar
photograph

On the way home from Dad's I take as many photos as I can:
Naked branches and tree trunks.
Fallen leaves.
A little girl falling asleep in her mother's arms on the bus.
The hands of a man holding on to the pole.
The blur of buildings and houses as we drive by.
Frank's Corner Store.
Lee Lee's house.
The street sign at the corner of my block.
The door to my house.
And before I go inside, I turn the camera on me.

19

libros
books

"This place feels magical," I say to Maxine. When she first told me she was bringing me to a bookstore, I wasn't that excited to go. But Powell's isn't just any bookstore. It's a massive haven that sells any book you can think of. There are so many rooms and floors, they give you a map. I've never ever heard of a bookstore giving you a map so you can get through it. We go to the art section, which is not a section but a whole room.

A short tan woman with a kinky Afro walks over to us. "Can I help you with anything?"

"Hi," Maxine says. "This is Jade. She's an artist—a collagist— and we're looking for some books for inspiration that show the work of black collagists."

Afro Woman says, "Oh, so you're an artist?" She starts walking fast through the aisles. "What do you make art about?" She turns down an aisle, starts slowing down, and then stops when we get to the middle.

I tell her all the things I love making art about.

"Well, I have the perfect books for you," she says. She pulls a book off the shelf. "Have you heard of Romare Bearden? He's one of the greats. You'll love his collages." We walk to another aisle, in search of more books. Afro Woman scans the shelves. "Ah, here we go." She pulls out another book. "This is a small collection of work from the artist Mickalene Thomas," she says. "She does mixed-media collages."

"This is gorgeous," Maxine says. She hands me the book.

I look through the pages. I have never seen art like this before—not in a book.

Afro Woman walks us to another aisle. "Yeah, Mickalene used to live in Portland," she tells us. I don't hear all of what she is saying because I am looking through the book, staring at these brown women and their faces that are pieced together with different shades of brown, different-size features, all mismatched yet perfectly puzzled together to make them whole beings. "I want to do this," I say out loud. They don't hear me because they are too busy talking about Mickalene and where she went to school and where she lived in Portland.

The whole way to the cashier, I am trying to choose which book to get now and which one to come back for. When we get in line, Maxine takes both books and says, "Anything else you want?"

Is that a trick question? I say no.

She pays for the books.

I can't stop thanking Maxine. She says, "You are more than welcome. Just thank me by making some great art."

Once we're in the car, I feel bad because we're not talking much. Seems like we should be getting to know each other. But the whole way home all I can do is stare at these masterpieces, study the making of me.

20

There are twelve girls who've been selected for the Woman to Woman mentorship program.

Twelve seeds.

Twelve prayers.

Twelve daughters.

Twelve roots.

Twelve histories.

Twelve reasons.

Twelve rivers.

Twelve questions.

Twelve songs.

Twelve smiles.

Twelve yesterdays.

Twelve tomorrows.

21

mujer a mujer

woman to woman

Being part of Woman to Woman is like having twelve new aunts. The way they all ask, "And how's school?" then "Any boys trying to get with you?" The way one is good for advice about choosing the right college and another is good for advice about choosing the right shade of makeup to complement your complexion.

Tonight's gathering is at Sabrina's house. "It's girl talk night," Sabrina says. She is sitting crossed-legged on the living room floor. The hardwood is shiny, like she mopped before we came. All twelve girls and all twelve mentors are here, and it doesn't even feel crowded. I think about all of us trying to squeeze into my house, how we'd bulge out of every corner like chubby feet in too-tight shoes. I hope tonight's topic is "How to Get a House Like Sabrina's." That's what I want to know how to do.

Most girls are on the floor, but I got here early, so I have a seat on one of the sofas. Everywhere I turn, I see snacks. Bowls of popcorn drizzled with olive oil and pepper. There is dried edamame in a small dish, and chocolate-covered sunflower seeds in a square bowl. The colorful, tiny seeds look like miniature Easter eggs. In the kitchen, fresh grapefruit slices float in a water cooler. I like plain water better, so I took some from the faucet before I sat down. "Help yourself to the snacks," Sabrina says. "Healthy living is healthy eating." There's a tray of vegetables in the center of the coffee table with a small bowl of hummus for dipping.

"We'll have one of these girl talk sessions once a quarter," Sabrina tells us. "Each time there will be a different topic."

Tonight's topic is dating. Sabrina asks each mentee to write one or two questions on the blank pieces of paper and put them in the question box.

I don't write a question.

I can tell by the looks on everyone's faces who's excited about talking about dating and who's terrified. Tamar literally sighs out loud, like she'd rather be anywhere but here. I see Ryan nudge her, telling her to pull it together. The twelve of us fit into four categories. Since Kayla is dating a guy who's in college and Tamar and Ryan are sitting here looking like they could lead this session, I put them in the "I Know Everything There Is to Know about Relationships" crew. Tracey, Ivy, Tameka, and Gabriella are in the "I'm Focused on School and I Don't Have Time for Anyone Else" group. I guess

I'm in that category too. I mean, I don't mind talking about dating, but it seems like every time adults have something to say to girls it's about what kind of boy not to talk to, what not to do with a boy. And even when they ask about our grades, and we tell them we have good grades, they usually say something like, "Well, that's good. I'm glad you're not distracted by them boys."

The only girls who seem excited by this discussion are Mercy, Sadie, and Lexus. They are the curious girls. They've dated before but have so much to learn. And then there's Jasmine. She's the only "I'm Saving Myself for Marriage" girl. Right now, Jesus is her boyfriend.

Sabrina says, "I've asked each mentor to come prepared to share the things they wish someone had told them about dating when they were your age."

Sabrina looks at Melanie. "Who wants to start?" she asks, when clearly she wants Melanie to speak first.

Melanie crosses her legs. She is one of the oldest mentors of the group. Midforties, I think. She is married, and talks about her husband like he's her favorite everything. "Sure, I'll give it a go," she says. "When I first got Sabrina's e-mail, I thought, well, if I'm really honest with myself, the truth is I was given some very good advice about dating. I just didn't listen."

The women laugh in agreement.

"Seriously," she says. "My mom schooled me well. She told me that before thinking about dating and sex and all of that, I needed to worry about myself because I would never be able to love anyone or treat anyone with dignity if I didn't first love and respect myself."

Rachel, one of the mentors, snaps her fingers like she's at a poetry café. "Girl, you can say that again!"

All the women are nodding, their heads moving like synchronized swimmers.

Tamar asks, "But what if you already know who you are and what you want?"

Another woman speaks. She looks at Tamar and says, "You think you know yourself, but trust me: you will keep growing and developing. That's why you all need to take the pressure off yourselves to have these serious relationships. You will change so much in the next ten years—"

Sabrina interrupts. "In ways you can't even imagine."

"Right," the woman says.

Ryan looks like she has checked out of the conversation. She is playing with the chocolate-covered sunflower seeds. Lining them up on her plate according to color.

Sabrina speaks again. "Any other mentors want to add something?" she asks.

Maxine hasn't spoken. She is looking all over the room, everywhere except Sabrina's direction, like she doesn't want to be called out. She must be thinking of Jon. Must be thinking she has no advice to give.

Brenda speaks. "I guess I'll add that relationships should be fun. I mean, there should be real joy in spending time with the person you are dating—and actually, this goes for friendships, too. If a person is making you the brunt of the joke all the time, or if they are dismissive of your feelings, then you need to stop wasting your time."

"Now that's the truth!" someone says.

Then Sabrina says, "With that, we'll go to the question box." She shakes the velvet box and pulls an index card out. "Our first question is, 'How do I get guys to notice me?'"

"I'll take that one," Carla says. "I think being yourself will attract the person who's best for you. You have to be true to yourself. Don't change what makes you *you*, because someone is going to want you. And the guys who don't, well, that's their loss."

The next question Sabrina pulls out says, *How do you get over someone you love?*

I don't mean to but I immediately look at Maxine. She looks away quickly when our eyes almost connect. I wonder how it feels to be here as a person who's supposed to have it all together but has some of the same questions that we do.

Melanie says, "Getting over someone is hard. You will think your heart will always be broken, but the truth is—it won't always hurt this bad."

Sabrina ends the night with a talk about following our dreams and believing in ourselves. "You have to believe you are worthy of love, of happiness. That you are worthy of your wildest dreams coming true."

When she says this, so many thoughts rush through my mind. I am thinking about how Mom had plenty of dreams, and

E.J. is not short on self-confidence, and Lee Lee has known she wants to be a poet since we were in middle school, so it can't be just about believing and dreaming. My neighborhood is full of big dreamers. But I know that doesn't mean those dreams will come true.

I know something happens between the time our mothers and fathers and teachers and mentors send us out into the world telling us, "The world is yours," and "You are beautiful," and "You can be anything," and the time we return to them.

Something happens when people tell me I have a pretty face, ignoring me from the neck down. When I watch the news and see unarmed black men and women shot dead over and over, it's kind of hard to believe this world is mine.

Sometimes it feels like I leave home a whole person, sent off with kisses from Mom, who is hanging her every hope on my future. By the time I get home I feel like my soul has been shattered into a million pieces.

Mom's love repairs me.

Whenever Mom's cooking is simmering on the stove and E.J.'s music is filling every inch of the house and I am making my art, I believe everything these women are saying about being worthy of good things. Those are the times I feel secure, feel just fine. I look in the mirror and see my dad's eyes looking back at me, my mom's thick hair, thick everything. And that's when I believe my dark skin isn't a curse, that my lips and hips, hair and nose don't need fixing. That my dream of being an artist and traveling the world isn't foolish.

Listening to these mentors, I feel like I can prove the negative stereotypes about girls like me wrong. That I can and will do more, be more.

But when I leave? It happens again. The shattering.

And this makes me wonder if a black girl's life is only about being stitched together and coming undone, being stitched together and coming undone.

I wonder if there's ever a way for a girl like me to feel whole.

Wonder if any of these women can answer that.

22

almorzar
to have lunch

Sam and I are walking from the bus stop to school. She is talking nonstop asking about Friday and Saturday and Sunday like it isn't only Monday morning. "Can you come over this weekend, or do you have something to do with Woman to Woman?" Sam asks me.

"Sorry, can't."

"Am I going to have to find a new best friend?" Sam asks.

I feel bad that I don't have any time to hang out with Sam. We only spend time together on the bus or at lunch. Every now and then we do our homework at Daily Blend, a coffee shop not too far from her house. We usually split a pastry and order iced coffees. Sometimes the owner gives us free refills.

We splash our way through the puddles, and as we enter St. Francis I see Glamour Girl pulling her car into the student parking lot. I've actually had to stop calling her Glamour Girl, because Sam gets confused and can't keep a straight face whenever someone says her real name, so I call her Kennedy now. Kennedy waves, and I wave back and hurry into the building to get out of the rain.

"See you at lunch," Sam says.

"Okay." I go to my locker, take off my wet coat, and pull the heavy books out of my backpack.

I can hear Kennedy coming because her laugh fills the hallway. She is walking with Josiah. "Lunch at Zack's?" Josiah says, to everyone in the hallway, it seems. He looks at me. "No excuses this time. Kennedy is driving."

I say okay, but only because E.J. gave me some money. He does that sometimes after he's deejayed at a big event.

Kennedy gives me half a smile and says, "Good morning." She searches through her junkyard of a locker and finally pulls out a book. "Jade, I didn't know you walked to school. I can give you a ride," she says.

"Oh, I don't walk. I take the bus."

She looks confused. "The bus? Where do you live?"

"North Portland," I tell her.

"*Oh,*" Kennedy says, like all kinds of lightbulbs are flashing in her head. "That makes *so* much sense now." She slams her locker and walks away. "See you at lunch," she says.

"Okay," I say. Even though now I'm not even sure I want to go.

23

reír

to laugh

Sam and I eat with Kennedy, Josiah, and two of their friends. I have no idea how six of us are going to fit into this car. When we get to the car, one of the girls, the only other white girl with us besides Sam, looks me over and says, "Um, maybe you should sit in the front," knowing my wide hips would take up too much space in the backseat.

When we get to Zack's Burgers, they are impatient with the woman who is taking our order, and so rude to her when she gets it wrong and brings Kennedy regular fries instead of sweet potato fries. Kennedy has a small tantrum because we don't have time to wait for a fresh batch, and the whole ride back she whines about how she's wasting her calories on something she doesn't really want.

And the other girl talks so bad about Northeast Portland, not knowing she is talking about Sam's neighborhood. Not knowing you shouldn't ever talk about a place like it's unlivable when you know someone, somewhere lives there. She goes on and on about how dangerous it used to be, how the houses are small, how it's supposed to be the new cool place, but in her opinion, "it's just a polished ghetto." She says, "God, I'd be so depressed if I lived there."

Kennedy and the other girls agree.

"That would be the worst thing ever," the white girl says. "I so don't understand how anyone could be happy there."

"Me either. I'd be so depressed."

If they feel that way about Sam's neighborhood, they must think I live in a wasteland.

Josiah is eating his food and staying out the conversation. Sam doesn't say anything the whole ride, but I can feel her eyes burning my back. When we get out, we barely say thanks for the ride, barely say good-bye to any of them. We sit in the hallway and eat our lunch. Sam and I on one side, Kennedy and the girls on the other. Josiah's gone to the computer lab because he gobbled his food down by the time we got back to St. Francis.

Sam swallows a mouthful of her burger and then whispers, "I'd be so depressed if I lived over here."

"Me too."

"I don't care that Kennedy has a car. I never want to do this again," Sam says.

"Me neither." I eat a handful of fries.

"But we have to go back to Zack's," Sam says.

And then we jinx each other. "This burger is so good," we say.

We laugh, our mouths full. Kennedy and her friends look over at us. They don't know why we're laughing so hard. Don't understand our joy.

24

tener hambre
to be hungry

When I get home, there's a note from Mom by the phone, along with a twenty-dollar bill. The note tells me to get something for dinner because she has a doctor's appointment. I decide on Dairy Queen so I can get a Blizzard—who cares if it's cold outside? I stop by Lee Lee's on my way, but she's not home, so I get on the bus and go by myself. Even though it's not late, it's dark and I don't really like to walk in the dark by myself. But tonight I don't have a choice.

Fall leaves cover the ground. Soon they will be trampled on by trick-or-treaters. Halloween is next weekend. Carved pumpkins sit on porches, their faces lit and haunting. And on the door outside the costume store there's a mummy holding a COSTUMES ON SALE sign.

The line at Dairy Queen is backed up all the way to the door, and it's hard to tell who has ordered already and who hasn't. There's a woman holding on to her toddler's hand while fussing with her other child, who looks about five, telling him to stop touching the dirty table that's coated with days-old ketchup. A group of boys are sitting at a table, all spread out and loud like they are eating at home in their dining room.

"You order yet?" a man asks me. He counts the single dollar bills in his hands, looks at the menu, and then counts again.

"Not yet," I tell him. I order my meal and step to the side so the man behind me can order. I hear the boys at the table, laughing and talking about who they would date and who they wouldn't. The guy in the light-blue shirt says, "What about Mercedes?"

And the rest of the group laughs and shakes their heads in fits of protest. One of them says, "Man, Mercedes's breath smells worse than your shoes!"

Then the one wearing a green hat adds, "And she got too much attitude."

They go on with their *what about*s, naming girls who are nowhere in sight, but then they start pointing at women who are in the restaurant. "What about her?" Green Hat says.

"Oh, she's a ten. Perfect ten."

They all agree that the next girl is a seven, and just when my order is ready, I hear one of them say, "What about her?"

I know he is pointing to me, which means they are all looking at me—from behind. Not good. The man at the counter calls my number and gives me my food.

The boys behind me assess me. One of them says, "I give her a five."

The other: "A five? Man, she so big, she breaks the scale."

Another voice: "Man, thick girls are fine. I don't know what's wrong with you."

"Well, if she so fine, go talk to her."

The man behind the counter looks at me, shakes his head, and says, "Boys."

I force a smile.

"Have a good evening," he says.

I wonder if any of these boys ever sit in a room for boys' talk night and discuss how to treat women. Who teaches them how to call out to a girl when she's walking by, minding her own business? Who teaches them that girls are parts—butts, breasts, legs—not whole beings?

I was going to eat at Dairy Queen, but I don't want to sit through the discussion of if I'm a five or not. I eat a few fries before I walk out.

"Hey, hold up. My boy wants to talk to you," Green Hat says. He follows me, yelling into the dark night.

I keep walking. Don't look back.

"Aw, so it's like that? Forget you then. Don't nobody want your fat ass anyway. Don't know why you up in a Dairy Queen. Need to be on a diet." He calls me every derogatory name a girl could ever be called.

I keep walking. Don't look back.

When I get on the bus, it is fuller than I expected it to be. I want to eat, but I decide to wait. Who wants to see a big girl eating fries and a burger on a bus? By the time I am home, my fries are cold, but the burger is still good. I don't throw the bag away. I'm going to use it tonight. Tear it up and make it into something. Maybe a dress for a girl more confident than I am, who doesn't feel insecure about eating whatever she wants in public. Maybe I'll morph it into a crown for the queen Dad says I am.

25

llamar
to name

The crown is in the center. It is not a princess crown. Not dainty
and sweet. In the background, the names he could have called
me emerge:
Hija
Amiga
Erudita
Artista
Soñador
. . .
Daughter
Friend
Scholar
Artist
Dreamer

26

el barrio
the neighborhood

"Okay, so tell me again: what stop do I get off at?" Sam asks.

I repeat the directions to her, part of me not believing she's really coming. After the fuss her grandma gave, I never thought she'd go anywhere past Lombard and MLK.

"Can you meet me at the bus stop? I told my grandparents you'd meet me and walk me back."

I want to say no. I want to say, *If you don't feel safe coming to my house, then don't come.* But instead I say, "Sure," because I know Sam really wants to come and I know she wouldn't be so scared if her grandma hadn't polluted her mind with all those stories.

I time the ride and leave to meet Sam. I zip my jacket, pull my hood over my head. October is gone and November has settled in. Not a lot of rain this month, but cloudy, cold, and gray, always.

Sam is not on the first bus, and for one moment—just one—I think, *What if something happened to her?* The whole story plays out in my mind—she will be on the news every day because she is a white girl and white girls who go missing always make the news. I will volunteer and join the other searchers. We will search all the many places a body could be. Cathedral Park. Some hidden bush under the St. John's bridge. For months people will tell girls and women to be careful and walk in pairs, but no one will tell boys and men not to rape women, not to kidnap us and toss us into rivers. And it will be a tragedy only because Sam died in a place she didn't really belong to. No one will speak of the black and Latino girls who die here, who are from here.

A bus screeches to a stop. I swallow those thoughts, watch the passengers exit the bus, and then I see Sam getting off at the back, smiling her Sam-smile.

We walk to Frank's. "Jade, my friend, where have you been?" Frank asks. He grabs the silver tongs and begins putting JoJos into a small white bag. I can tell he just made them. The potato wedges have that crisp, golden look that I like. He throws a few packets of ketchup in the bag.

"I've been busy with school," I tell him. "By the time I come home, you're closed."

"That's good, that's good," he says. He begins putting chicken wings into another white bag. "Four?"

"Yes, please."

He nods and puts in a few extra.

Sam walks over to the aisle of chips.

Frank whispers, "How you liking it out there with all them white folks?"

"It's all right," I tell him.

"Good, good."

Sam returns with a bag of Doritos. I hand them to Frank and give him money. He waves his hand in the air. "It's on the house today," he says. "Tell your mom I said hello. Haven't seen her in a while either."

"I will," I say. "Thanks for this." I take the food and walk away.

As I'm going out the door, Lee Lee is coming in. "I just left your house. E.J. said you should be back soon," she says. She reaches out to hug me. I hug her back and smell the hair grease and the fruity lotion she uses all in one. "Feels like I haven't seen you in forever," Lee Lee says.

"I know. I came by the other night, but you weren't home," I tell her.

"Don't even try to put this on me. You're the one who has to take a canoe, a plane, and a bus to school. If you would be regular, I'd be seeing you every day." Lee Lee barely gets her joke out, she's laughing so hard. Then she finally notices that I am not alone, and she pulls her laugh in.

"This is Sam," I tell her.

"Finally!" Lee Lee opens her arms wide like she's known Sam forever. They hug. She's good with anybody who's good with me and vice versa.

"Nice to meet you," Sam says.

"What are you two about to do?" Lee Lee asks.

"Nothing. Just going back to my house."

Lee Lee walks the aisles and gets a candy bar and a soda. After she pays, we walk out together. "You want to go to Andrea's? Kobe is there," she says. Lee Lee and Andrea are cousins. They've lived together since we were in middle school, but Lee Lee always calls it Andrea's house. Kobe is their cousin too. He might as well live there. Every time I go over, he's there or on his way or just leaving.

Sam and I eat the JoJos on the way. Lee Lee gulps her soda. When we get to Andrea's house, her mom points toward the door at the end of a long hallway. "They in there," she says. Andrea and Kobe are in her bedroom, listening to music. When they see me, they start screaming like I'm some celebrity or something.

"Jade!" Andrea is the first one to hug me. She is wearing jeans and a shirt, but somehow she still looks stylish. Her makeup is flawless—foundation, eye shadow, mascara, lip gloss. Her weave is long. A mixture of blond and brown wavy hair. Andrea holds on to me, and when she lets go, she asks, "Where have you been?"

"She's been handling her business!" Kobe says. He kisses me on both cheeks. "How's my girl?" he asks.

"I'm good, Kobe. How are you?"

"Girl, you know me—I stay fabulous," he says. "And who do we have here?" He looks Sam up and down.

"This is my friend Sam. She goes to my school."

Kobe hugs her and then reaches for the plastic grocery bag in my hand. "What you got up in there?"

I take out one of the chicken wings and pass the bag. He takes one, grabs a napkin, and gives the bag to Andrea.

The five of us feast on corner store food.

Sam says, "So do you all go to the same school?"

Andrea, Kobe, and Lee Lee nod. Andrea says, "We go to Northside. I like it there. I mean, it's not like St. Francis, you know." She looks at me. "We're not traveling the world and learning a million languages."

Kobe laughs. "How many languages do you speak now, Jade?"

"Don't do that," I say. "I'm only learning one other language."

Andrea swallows a handful of chips. "French?" she asks.

Lee Lee jumps in. "You know Jade is all about Spanish. Do you guys remember when we were in elementary school and Jade said she wanted to go to Sesame Street and speak Spanish with Maria and Luis and work in the Fix-It Shop?"

They laugh at me and I laugh too.

"She was like, 'I'm going to travel the world and be rich and buy my mom a big house.' Remember that?" Lee Lee asks.

"That's still the goal," I tell them.

Lee Lee looks at Sam and says, "But for real, there's not much to say about Northside. We don't have all the electives you do at St. Francis. The only club worth mentioning is the after-school poetry club. It's kind of DIY though."

Sam says, "DIY?"

"Yeah, it's not really an official club or anything. My English teacher, Mrs. Baker, lets us use her room after school to write poems. There's no teacher; we just kind of meet up and write and then share."

"That's pretty cool," Sam says.

Lee Lee reaches for a pillow and props it against her back. "Not as cool as having a garden on your rooftop, and cooking classes."

"Well, yeah, but I don't know many teachers at St. Francis who would let us stay in their classrooms and write poems. I mean, they'd make it so formal that they'd take the fun out of it. You know? It really would have to become a club or an after-school class with a staff adviser and blah, blah, blah. No freedom to just be, you know?"

"She's right," I tell them, just to be sure Lee Lee, Kobe, and Andrea know Sam isn't trying to make them feel better about Northside. "Lee Lee's poems are so good, she could probably teach the class," I tell Sam.

Lee Lee smiles. Big, like she needed to hear that.

Andrea turns the music up a little and says, "This is my song!" and that gets us all singing and listening to music for the rest of the afternoon.

When it's time for Sam to go home, she takes her cell phone out and calls her grandfather to let him know she's on her way.

Lee Lee gives me a look and says, "You're walking her to the bus stop? I'll go too."

We say our good-byes to Andrea and Kobe, and leave.

As we walk to the bus stop, Lee Lee says to Sam, "So, did you just move to Portland?"

"Me? Oh, no. I was born at Emanuel Hospital. I've lived in Portland my whole life."

"Oh," Lee Lee says, her brows scrunched in a fit of confusion. "So why— So where do you live?"

"Northeast Portland. Not too far from Peninsula Park."

Lee Lee doesn't ask any more questions. She keeps walking. We make it to the bus stop just as the bus is pulling up.

"See you," Sam says.

We wave and say good-bye.

On the way home, I tell Lee Lee what Sam's grandma said about North Portland. "That's why I walked her to the bus stop," I say. "To make her grandparents comfortable."

Lee Lee laughs. She says, "White people are a trip."

"What do you mean?"

"I can't believe her grandparents are scared to let her come over here. There are a lot of white people who live over here. Don't they know that?" she asks. "And maybe they don't know—but Northeast has its sketchy streets still. It hasn't changed over there *that* much." Lee Lee shakes her head. "How you gonna live in a 'hood but be afraid to come to another 'hood?" she asks.

We laugh about that the whole way home.

27

agradecido
thankful

For Thanksgiving, Mom and I do our annual tradition. This time E.J. and Lee Lee join us. We go downtown and volunteer at the Portland Rescue Mission. "We don't have much, but we have more than a lot of other people," Mom says.

I hope one day my family gets to a place where we can be thankful just to be thankful and not because we've compared ourselves to someone who has less than we do.

After we're done dishing out turkey dinners with all the holiday fixings, we eat dinner at my house. Mom made ham with her not-so-secret ingredient of brown sugar, and all the traditional sides are spread across the table. Everything looks so good, you'd never know this wasn't some fancy dining room table holding it all up.

As we eat, Lee Lee says, "My teacher Mrs. Phillips doesn't celebrate Thanksgiving. Can you believe that?"

Mom puts her fork down. "Why not? She doesn't have anything to be thankful for?"

E.J. swallows and says, "Oh, Mrs. Phillips—I remember her. She's that revolutionary-activist-fight-the-power teacher at Northside. I loved her class," he says. "I remember her telling us that Thanksgiving should actually be a national day of mourning or something like that."

Lee Lee nods. "That's exactly what she says."

"What does that even mean?" Mom asks.

E.J. answers, "Basically, we're sitting here feasting and celebrating that our nation was stolen from indigenous people. Columbus didn't discover nothing."

All of a sudden my food doesn't taste as good as before.

Mom wipes her mouth with her napkin. "I've never thought about it like that. Thanksgiving has always been a day for getting together with family, a day to thank God for my personal blessings. But, well, I guess your teacher has a point." Mom takes another bite of food.

Lee Lee says, "Yeah, Mrs. Phillips is always asking us to think about other perspectives. Next week we're having a cultural exchange with teens who attend a program at the Native American Youth and Family Center."

"I think we went there, too." E.J. says. "And they came over to the rec."

I feel so embarrassed that I've never even thought about any of this. Never realized that there was a community center for Native American youth here in Portland. Mom, E.J., and Lee Lee keep on talking, comparing the experience of African Americans and Native Americans in the United States. I don't even know what was said to make E.J. get all fired up. He's talking like he's in a debate. "I mean, I get all of that—the US has done some messed-up things. But I'd rather live here than any other country. Real talk. I feel what Mrs. Phillips is saying and everything, but at the end of the day, we still got a lot to be thankful for living here."

Mom takes a bite of food, then says, "Jade, you're mighty quiet over there. What do you think?"

"Me?" I take a moment to get my thoughts together. "I guess, well, you're all right. I think the US has a lot to be thankful for *and* a lot to apologize for."

The rest of dinner is more somber than usual. The mood doesn't lighten up until Mom brings out the peach cobbler that Lee Lee and I made. It's the first time we've ever baked anything from scratch. Mom dishes out cobbler for each of us. I watch her as she takes her first bite. "You like it?" I ask.

"Mmm-hmm," she says, even though the look on her face says she wants to spit it out.

E.J. gets a spoon and scoops out a bite. "Let me taste," he says. He blows on the spoon, all dramatic like it's burning hot, and then he puts it into his mouth. He swallows and looks at

Mom, who gives him her don't-start-nothing look, and then he says, "No comment."

Lee Lee hits him on the arm. "Forget you. Next time you make dessert."

"Next time let's just get ice cream from Safeway."

We all end up laughing, and the night ends with card games and Scrabble, and I go to bed, full in so many, many ways.

28

las diferencias
differences

It's the first weekend of December. The rain is steady and the air is cold. Maxine honks her horn for me to come out. I get into her car and am greeted by the blowing heat. It feels like a sauna in here.

We drive downtown, to the Portland Art Museum. "Have you been to a museum before?" Maxine asks.

"Does OMSI count?"

"Kind of. Well, not really. I mean, OMSI is interactive, so it's not the same as traditional museums. That's what makes it so unique. Where we're going today is, like, well, I don't know. It might be different than what you've experienced. Like, you can't touch the art and you won't be able to take photos, and it's a really quiet space, so we'll have to talk softly."

I feel like she thinks I don't know how to act in public or

something. "Okay, got it," I say. I look out the window. The weeping clouds drench the ground. Maxine turns her windshield wipers to a faster speed.

When we get to the museum, we meet up with the rest of the group. Sabrina repeats some of the same rules Maxine told me in the car. She gives us a time to meet back at this spot. "Have fun," she says.

As we enter the first exhibit, Maxine's phone rings. "Give me a sec," she says. She walks away from me and answers her phone. "Jon?"

I stand to the side of the entrance. Ten minutes pass. I go to find Maxine. She is outside, standing in front of the building.

When she sees me, she mouths, *I'm so sorry. This is important.* She shoos me off with her hand. "Go ahead. Go in without me."

I stand there for a moment. "Are you sure?"

She nods.

I walk away. I wonder what they have to talk about. I mean, when you break up with someone, it's over. That's it. What's left to discuss over and over? And why do these conversations have to happen when Maxine is with me? For all the things about Maxine that I respect and admire, there are things like this that make me feel like she can't really tell me anything about loving myself and taking care of myself because here she is, doing the opposite.

I walk around the museum and bump into another mentee-mentor pair who are taking photos even though there's a sign that says no photographs are allowed.

"Hey, Miss Jade," Brenda calls out. "Where's Maxine?"

"On the phone. Outside." I don't try to hide my frustration.

Brenda makes a confused face but doesn't say anything. "You can join us," she says.

We walk through the museum, but I can't even really enjoy it. I feel like I'm intruding on their time, and I can't stop thinking how rude it was for Maxine to take that phone call—especially from Jon.

I stray from Brenda and Jasmine and walk through the photograph collection. I have walked through most of the exhibits when I see Sabrina, who tells me it's time to meet up at the front so we can reflect. We're all supposed to say one thing we enjoyed and one question we have. I skip out on the closing to go to the bathroom.

When I come out of the restroom, Maxine is sitting on a bench in the lobby. "So sorry about that. We had to have that conversation," she says.

I don't say anything. I can't even fake a that's-okay smile.

"Well, I feel terrible that we didn't spend time together. How about I take you to dinner?"

I don't really want to say yes, but I'm hungry and I know there aren't many options for dinner at home.

"Let's walk to someplace close," she says. On the way to the restaurant, Maxine does most of the talking, because I don't really have anything to say to her, plus it's hard to walk and talk at this pace, going uphill. I'll be out of breath if I say too much. "So, what did you think?" she asks.

I want to tell her that I think she should have called Jon back later. That I think I should be important too. But I know there's only one answer she's looking for. "It was awesome. I loved it."

"I'm glad you enjoyed it. You know, this city has so much to offer, so much great art to see. People just stay in their bubble of North Portland and never get out to see all that the city has," she says. "Have your friends ever been here?"

I know she is not referring to my friends at St. Francis but the ones in my neighborhood. "Probably," I say. Even though I am not sure.

When we get to the restaurant, there's a short wait and then we are seated. Once we've had time to look the menu over, the waitress approaches the table. Maxine orders grilled salmon on top of arugula and an Arnold Palmer. She says to me, "Get whatever you want, okay?"

I really want a burger and fries but I don't want a Healthy Eating, Healthy Living lecture right now. So, even though I've never had arugula and I have no idea what an Arnold Palmer is, I order the same thing as Maxine.

When the meal comes, I realize that an Arnold Palmer is some weird name for lemonade and iced tea mixed together. It's actually pretty good. So is the salmon and arugula. Maxine starts with the small talk, but I can't muster the fakeness. I am still thinking about what she said on our way here. "What did you mean when you said people in North Portland live in a bubble? I live in North Portland and I—"

"Oh, no—not you specifically. I meant that I know a lot of people who only stay within the small confinement of their blocks. They don't really go out of their neighborhood to explore other areas." Maxine squeezes a lemon into her drink.

I'm not trying to be disrespectful to Maxine, but I don't like her talking about my friends like she knows them, like she understands anything about them. "Maybe they can't afford these places," I tell her.

"Yes, well, maybe the museum is a little pricey," Maxine says. "But I think they have special discounts for families who can't afford full admission. All that kind of info is on their website."

"Well, not every family has a computer and, if they do, they might not have the Internet," I tell her.

Maxine is full of ideas. "There are a lot of free things too. I mean, even taking a drive to Multnomah Falls or going to Bonneville Dam."

"Yeah, well, my mom doesn't have a car, so there goes that idea," I say. "And if she did, I'm sure she'd need to be conservative on where to drive in order to keep gas in the car."

Maxine shakes her head at me. "Always the pessimist," she says, laughing.

Always the realist, I think. *Always the poorest.*

Maxine goes on talking, not even realizing she's so oblivious. We've been at the restaurant so long that most of the people who were here when we first came in are gone and a whole new crowd has come.

"How's your mom?" Maxine asks.

"She's good. Working a lot," I say.

"And what is it she does again?"

Again? I never told her. I tell Maxine about my mom working for Ms. Louise. "And now she's working for another woman on the weekends."

Even though this is good news, Maxine's eyes are full of pity. She sounds like those annoying adults who take babies by the hand and talk in gibberish, in that childish voice. "So many people can't find work in this economy," she says. "Your mom is lucky."

I think, *She is not lucky*. She works hard. Figured out a way to keep the lights on and the bills paid. Didn't give up. All this talk about my mom makes me wonder about Maxine's family. I ask her, "What about your mother? What does she do?"

"She's a surgeon," Maxine says.

"So she must have been at work a lot when you were younger too?"

"She was, actually. Yeah, she was."

"Did you have a mentor?"

"No. I didn't," Maxine tells me.

I wonder why people didn't think Maxine needed a mentor. Wonder why Maxine thinks she can be a mentor if she's never had one.

The waitress asks if we need anything else before leaving the bill. Maxine says no and pulls out her wallet.

"Any other questions for me?" Maxine asks.

I wait for the waitress to walk away and then I say, "Yes. What makes you want to do this?"

"Well, I guess I'm doing this because, well, because I want to make a difference and because I—"

I roll my eyes. "The real reason," I tell her. "Is it good money? Did you always want a little sister? There has to be a reason."

Maxine laughs. "Okay, here it is—the money does help, of course. And, um, let's see, well, I'm really interested in working with young girls and women—especially women of color—in regards to their mental, physical, and emotional health. So I thought this would be a good experience for me," Maxine tells me.

"But why?" I ask. "I mean, what makes you want to do something like that?"

The waitress comes back with chocolate mints and the receipt. Maxine signs her name. "I guess I'm doing it because I could have used someone helping me out when I was your age. It would have been nice to have someone to talk to."

"You think I need someone to talk to?" I ask.

"I don't know. Do you?"

It takes me a while to answer. Not because I don't need someone, but because I don't want to say yes and have her thinking my mom is not a good mother. I don't want her thinking I am some 'hood girl with a bunch of problems she has to come and fix.

"Jade, I know this is kind of awkward," Maxine says. "I mean, we're still getting to know each other. I know it's going to take time, but hopefully one day you'll feel like you can tell me anything."

I tune out some of what Maxine is saying because now it's starting to sound like something she practiced, something Sabrina told her to say. But when she says, "We're going to have so much fun with the other mentor-mentee pairs. I can't wait for us to grow and learn from each other."

I ask her, "How is that going to happen if you keep flaking out on the activities?"

Maxine looks stunned that I actually said this. She takes a sip of her Arnold Palmer even though there's not much left to drink. "You have every right to be upset with me for being so flaky today," Maxine says.

"And last month," I add.

"All I can say is I am sorry and, like I told you earlier, it won't happen again."

I don't say anything. I'm just sitting here, thinking how different we are. How I'm not sure why Mrs. Parker thought we'd be a good pair.

"You have my word, Jade," Maxine says. "I hope you'll give me another chance."

One more chance. That's all she's got.

29

la llorona

the weeping woman

I am on my way downtown to walk through the city and take photos. The bus is pretty empty when I get on. Only three people in the front—an elderly man and a mother with her young son, and a few teens near the back. I sit in the middle section and look out the window. The streets are as solemn as the sky. At the third stop a woman gets on the bus, her hair not so straight anymore because of the rain. She has on sandals and jeans that look like they've never been washed. Her shirt hangs so low and is so thin, you can see her braless breasts. She says to the driver, "Can I get on?"

He says, "Pay your fare, ma'am."

"I ain't got no fare. Can I get on? I'm just going a few blocks."

The driver sighs a long sigh. "Come on," he says.

The braless woman wobbles to the seat across from me. I try not to stare at her, but she makes it hard because she is mumbling to herself and crying. She is not an old woman or a young woman. She is not pretty or ugly. I wonder who loves her, who is worried about her, who maybe cared so much but had to give up on her. I wonder what she was like when she was my age. Did she ever think she'd be on a bus, drenched from the rain, smelling like sorrow and regret?

When I get off, she calls out, "Jesus loves you. Jesus loves you."

I walk around the city like I'm a tourist, my camera in hand. Every corner has a story; every block asks a question. So many worlds colliding all at once. I document my walk, hiding away in places people can't see me so I'm not obvious. I don't want anyone to pose or stop and ask why I'm taking their photo. I just want to capture the city. I put the setting on black-and-white and begin.

The line at Voodoo Doughnuts that wraps around the block.

The food carts on Alder Street.

The umbrella man at Pioneer Square.

The *Portlandia* statue.

The Portland marquee at the Arlene Schnitzer, its oversize lights framing the sign.

And then I see a mural I've never seen before. On the front of the old Oregon Historical Society building there's a larger-than-life mural of Lewis and Clark, Sacagawea with her baby, and York with Seaman, the dog that accompanied them on the trip. I have never seen this mural before. Never seen York alongside the others. They seem to be stepping out of the building. The four of them so high, they look over the city.

I take a few photos of the mural. And on the last one, I zoom in on York's face.

30

feliz navidad
Merry Christmas

Lee Lee and Sam come over to make holiday cards. Before we even get started, Lee Lee says, "I'm just here for moral support. Jade, you know I can't draw."

"You don't have to draw anything. We're making collages," I remind her.

"I'm not an artist like you, Jade," Lee Lee says, like she didn't even hear what I said.

"But look, the art is mostly done for you." I open the small plastic bin I have that's full of Christmas cards from last year. Some were given to me, some to my mom. I tore off the front of the cards and saved them so I could recycle them for this year. I do it with Valentine's Day cards too. I tell Lee Lee and Sam, "All you have to do is cut and paste. There's really no wrong way to do it."

"You must not remember sixth grade," Lee Lee says. We burst into laughter, so hard that I have to wipe tears from my eyes. Lee Lee explains it all to Sam. "Our art teacher kept giving the same we're-all-artists speech Jade is trying to give us, but when it came time for her to hang our self-portraits in the hallway for parent night, guess what she said to me." Lee Lee looks at me for me to take over.

I talk in Mrs. White's frail shaky voice, "Well, hmm. Well, let's see, Lenora, I think we just might set this one aside. I'll find a special place for it, but maybe, well, maybe it won't go on the bulletin board."

Lee Lee finishes, "Mrs. White never found a special place—well, the trash can, maybe. But it never made it to the bulletin board or anywhere on a wall in the classroom. I couldn't believe how shocked she sounded, like she had never, ever seen something so bad in all her years of teaching."

"And that didn't hurt your feelings?" Sam asks.

"Not at all. I know what I'm good at, and it ain't drawing or painting or cutting things up and making something out of them. That's Jade. I'm the poet."

I tell Sam, "We used to do each other's assignments. I would draw for Lee Lee, and she would write for me." I grab the scissors and cut out a Christmas tree.

"It worked until middle school, but then we met Mrs. White and there was no way to trick her. And so, left to my own skills, my self-portrait looked like I hated myself," Lee Lee says.

Sam laughs just a little until Lee Lee tells her, "It's okay. You can laugh at me. It's pretty pathetic, I know." Then Sam lets a real laugh out.

I hand a few cards to Lee Lee. "Cut things out," I tell her. "I'll design."

Lee Lee picks up a pair of scissors and starts cutting.

Sam grabs scissors and starts cutting too. "I can't believe you saved all of this. I throw cards away the minute I get them. Well, not like I get that many, but yeah. I don't keep anything."

We make cards for the rest of the afternoon, only stopping to make hot chocolate. Lee Lee is writing a poem for Mrs. Baker, and Sam is writing a note to her grandfather. I finished a card for my mom, but I haven't written anything yet. I'm working on one for Maxine. I'll write something later.

The room is full of the sound of scissors slicing and pens gliding across construction paper. Lee Lee puts her pen down and then says, "Sam, what are you good at? What do you like to do?"

Sam stops writing. She thinks—longer than I expect—and says, "I don't know. Nothing like writing poetry or making art. I'm just . . . I don't know. I don't really like making things as much as I like enjoying them; like, I mean, I'd rather read a story than write one. I'd rather go to a museum and see art than paint something," she tells us. "So pretty much, I'm lazy, I guess. And I have no talent." She laughs a little.

"Maybe that means you're good at listening," I say. I think

about all the conversations we've had, how Sam always looks at me like she is really focusing on my words, taking all of me in. How she is a good observer, always noticing my mood and asking if I'm okay. "You're a good friend," I tell her. "That's a talent."

"Sure is," Lee Lee says. "Not everyone knows how to be that." Lee Lee gets to talking about one of our friends who isn't really our friend anymore. She keeps saying she doesn't care, but you wouldn't know it by the way she keeps going on and on. It's almost like she isn't talking to me or Sam. Like she is caught in her own replay of how our ex–best friend kissed her boyfriend.

And while Lee Lee is reliving her heartache, Sam seems like she is in her own world too. Her face is stuck on a smile, her eyes bright and thankful. She looks at me and says almost in a whisper, "You're a good friend too."

31

víspera de Año Nuevo
New Year's Eve

I write my resolution in black Sharpie marker on top of a background made out of cut-up scriptures, words from newspaper headlines, and numbers from last year's calendar.

Be bold.

Be brave.

Be beautiful.

Be brilliant.

Be (your) best.

32

hermanas
sisters

Ever since my talk with Maxine, she's been making an effort to
spend time with me—and really be with me. Not late, not checking her phone. Tonight she invited me over to her apartment.
Mom took no time to say yes. A few of Maxine's friends are coming over, and she wants me to meet them. She picked me up early
enough to go to Safeway to get snacks: chocolate pretzels, cheese
and crackers, mixed nuts. She takes out serving dishes from the
cabinet, and I pour the pretzels and nuts into separate bowls
while she arranges the crackers around the chunk of cheese in
the middle of a small tray. "Thanks for helping," she says. She sets
the food out on the coffee table.

Maxine's apartment has two bedrooms, and each has its own
bathroom; plus there's a half bathroom, for guests, in the hallway. The living room, dining room, and kitchen blend into one

another in one big space, separated by furniture and appliances. There's a framed world map in the center of her living room wall, black-and-white photos to the left and right. One of the Eiffel Tower, the other the Brooklyn Bridge. Her living room looks like she bought a whole showroom at a furniture store—everything matching and perfectly in its place. "I love your apartment," I tell her.

"Thanks," Maxine says. "Don't open that closet, though," she says, laughing. "Have to have at least one messy space."

There's a knock on her door, and when Maxine opens it, two girls come in. "Max!" They exchange hugs and file in. Maxine introduces us. I make mental notes so I can remember their names. Bailey is the one who has hair braided in big thick cords and pinned back into a maze of rows that make a full bun at the back of her head. Kira is the one with straight hair, a light brown color like her eyes.

Bailey says, "It's nice to meet you. I've heard so much about you."

I smile and wonder what Maxine has told them.

Bailey and Kira sit in the living room. I join them.

Maxine pours iced tea and offers the snacks to everyone. "Eat up, ladies," she says.

Kira wastes no time getting to business. "So, lay it on us," Kira says. "What's the deal with you and Jon?"

"There's nothing to say. We broke up. That's it."

"He's trying to get back with her though," Bailey says. "Calls her a million and one times a day."

"You're not picking up, are you, Max? I mean, what does he have to say?" Kira asks.

"He still thinks he has access to her stuff. Didn't he ask to use your car the other day?" Bailey asks.

Maxine says, "That's not all he calls about. He called the other day to apologize. He said he was sorry for everything."

"Well, we know that," Kira says. "He's been sorry from day one—"

"Oh, come on," Maxine says. "None of us knew Jon was going to cheat on me. I mean, we had a good two-year relationship."

Bailey's voice is softer now, like she knows what she's about to say might hurt Maxine's feelings. "Max, Jon may not have been cheating on you that whole time, but, well, he was kind of using you. I mean, always needing your car, always asking for money—even if he didn't cheat, the writing was on the wall that the two of you didn't need to be together."

"Why? Because he lost his job? I'm not a gold digger. I didn't care that—"

"He got fired. That's not losing his job. He got fired because he kept showing up high and late," Kira says. "I mean, let's be honest."

I stuff my mouth with pretzels and listen to the soap opera tales of Jon and Maxine.

"All right—he had some issues. You can't help who you love. And besides, the point is, We. Broke. Up. Remember? I let him go," Maxine says.

Kira and Bailey say, almost in unison, "Just don't take him back."

Maxine looks at me. "I hope you have good friends to keep you from making stupid mistakes," she says. She sits next to me on the sofa.

"My friends wouldn't have let me date a guy like him in the first place," I tell her. "And *definitely* not my mom."

Maxine looks part offended, part surprised.

"Sorry. I didn't mean to—"

"No, it's fine. It's— Point well taken," she says. "And in Kira and Bailey's defense—they did try. But we had a history, and I couldn't walk away without trying to make it work. I tried. It didn't work. I'm moving on—trying to move on," Maxine says.

I feel bad that all we've talked about is Jon. I change the subject by asking them to tell me what college was like for them. Kira says, "Well, I'm still in college, actually. This is my last year at Portland State." Kira and Maxine talk to me about dorm life. Kira says, "Living on my own but still close to family was good for me. I needed that."

Bailey went to the University of San Diego. "My freshman year was so hard. But after I found my spots—where to get the hair products I like, a black church, you know, the essentials—I was good."

We talk till the sun is swallowed by the sky. We've devoured all of the snacks, so Maxine orders pizza from a gourmet pizza shop. When she asks what kind we want, everyone says things like feta and grilled chicken and basil, and Maxine asks, "What about tofu instead of chicken?" And I am sure this is going to be the nastiest pizza I've ever tasted.

While we wait for the delivery, the conversation stays on food. Maxine shares her newest smoothie recipes, and Bailey mentions how hard it's going to be to avoid chocolate with Valentine's Day right around the corner.

Bailey asks, "Speaking of V-Day. Anybody got plans?"

Kira rolls her eyes. "I know what I'm *not* going to do," she says. "I will not be attending the performance of *The Vagina Monologues* at PSU."

They all laugh.

Kira eats the last little crumbs of pretzels in the bowl. "I've really had enough. Every year the school puts this play on like it's the only play about the issues women face. I mean, what about *For Colored Girls?*"

Maxine says, "They are not going to do *For Colored Girls.*"

"They have before," Kira says. "A long time ago."

Bailey asks, "What's wrong with *The Vagina Monologues?*"

"Yeah," I say. "What is it about?"

Kira and Bailey look at Maxine and Maxine's eyes get big and I start feeling like I do whenever I know my mom doesn't want to tell me something.

Bailey stutters, "C-can she—"

"Um, it's a play that features stories about women. It, uh, it covers issues like love and relationships—" Maxine starts telling me.

"And rape, sex, getting your period for the first time," Kira interrupts.

"Okay, okay, I think she gets it," Maxine says.

Delivery comes, and once Maxine has brought the box into the kitchen, we all reach in to grab a slice.

Kira pours more iced tea for everyone. "Okay, so back to the conversation at hand. What's the big deal, talking about that play? What? Jade can't hear the word *sex*?"

"Kira!" Bailey throws a pillow at her.

The three of them go back and forth, debating over what I'm too young to know, what I'm old enough to talk about, and who should tell me.

I sit and eat my pizza. It's not as bad as I thought it would be. The sauce is really good, and there's a lot of it, so I barely taste the thin pieces of tofu.

I wonder if this is what having big sisters would be like. I have always wanted an older sister. When I was ten, I asked Mom if she would give me a sister for Christmas. I had no idea what I was really asking. She laughs about that now, telling me I asked Dad, too, and he actually considered it.

We end the night playing round after round of Taboo. We alternate teams until each of us has partnered. It is getting late, and Maxine calls it a night so she can take me home. While we are cleaning up the mess we made, Kira whispers to me, "For real, though, if you have questions about sex or anything Miss Prude Maxine won't talk with you about, let me know."

"Kira—please leave Jade alone. She is not like that. She's smart. She's on scholarship at St. Francis and has a four-point-oh GPA. This girl right here is going places. She's not going to mess things up by getting caught up with some guy," she says. "I'm going to see to it she doesn't end up like one of *those* girls."

I know when Maxine says *those girls*, she is talking about the girls who go to Northside. I don't know what to say. Every time I see Maxine, it is two steps forward, two steps back. Here I was, thinking how quickly it happened that I fit in with her friends and how we are easy with one another as if we have shared years of laughter. But then I think, how quick it is that Maxine reminds me that I am a girl who needs saving. She knows I want out and she has come with a lifeboat. Except I just don't know if I can trust her hand.

33

lo mismo
the same

I am finished with my first collage about York, Lewis, and Clark. Mom thinks I'm obsessed with their stories. I tell her, maybe I am. Tell her that it's interesting to me that a black man made the journey to find this place—the Pacific Northwest—when all I want to do is leave it. Mom says, "Just come back to me and visit every now and then."

Tonight I make something about a different expedition. The one I am on. I want to get out, and I feel like a traitor for admitting it.

Maxine is right and wrong.

Wrong because I *am* like *those* girls. I am the Kool-Aid–drinking, fast food–eating unhealthy girl she wants to give nutrition classes to. I know all about food stamps and dollar menus and layaway. Know how to hold my purse tight at night when walking down dark streets, know how to duck at the sound of a shooting gun. I do. I am the girl who walks down the hallway, hoping for at least one boy to notice me. But the boys at school don't like me because I look nothing like their mothers, look nothing like the Dream. The boys over here, well, to them I am good for tutoring and friendshipping and advice giving. I am.

So Maxine is wrong—so wrong—about me.

But she is also right, because I know more than that, want more than that. Right because I am the girl who spends her summers reading books and working, tutoring at the rec, when a lot of her friends are at the rec, playing their summers away. I am the girl who knows when to stop talking back to a teacher because I know my mother will be waiting for me when I get home, asking me if I forgot who raised me. I am the girl who dreams of going places: to college, to grad school, all around the world, if I can.

Maxine is right and wrong. *Those girls* are not the opposite of me. We are perpendicular. We may be on different paths, yes. But there's a place where we touch, where we connect and are just the same.

34

pertenecer
to belong

Life has only been school all day, tutoring afterward, and sad
looks from Sam, who thinks I have forgotten about her. I tell her
I haven't been hanging out with anyone, not even Lee Lee, and I
used to see her every day. She believes me, I think. But it doesn't
make her feel any better when I say, "Sorry, I can't come over."
Today, though, I don't have anything to do after school, so we
decide to go to Pioneer Place to shop. Well, Sam's shopping. I'm
just going.

Sam drags me in and out of stores for the rest of the afternoon. The only stores we go into are for skinny girls, so I'm
glad I don't have any money to buy anything. "Let's go in here,"
she says. We step into a store lit by bright lights and with music
so loud, we can barely hear each other talk. Sam stops at the
first rack and picks up a blue long-sleeved shirt that's thin and

low-cut. She holds it up to her torso and then tosses the shirt over her arm.

I have never been able to pick up a shirt, hold it up to my body, and know it can fit. I have to try everything on. Everything.

We walk to the next rack. "What about this skirt? Too short?"

I look at it, then look at the mannequin to see where it falls on her. "Um, it might be fine if you wear leggings under it."

Sam grabs a skirt in her size and adds it to the growing bundle on her arm. She goes rack to rack, deciphering jeans, shirts, and skirts. Her arms are so full that one of the salesclerks comes over to us and asks if she can start a room. She is white with curly red hair and freckles that can barely be seen unless you stand close to her. Her nails are painted emerald green and they match her leggings. "I'll put you in room four," she says. Sam continues to the back of the store. The woman looks at me. "Is there something I can help you with?"

I smile. "Thanks for asking, but I don't think there's one thing in here that could even fit my pinky toe, let alone my whole body." I am joking, but I guess she doesn't think I'm funny. She doesn't laugh or even smile.

She says, "We don't allow loitering in our store."

"Loitering? I'm just— I'm waiting for my friend."

"You are more than welcome to wait out there," she says, pointing to the bench sitting outside the entrance.

"So, I can't look around?"

"Well, of course, you can. But you can't stand idle and—"

I walk away. There's no point in arguing with her; plus I see a cute bag on sale in the back of the store. On my way to the bags, I get distracted by all the earrings. I try on a few pairs and then pick up a thick bracelet the color of a pomegranate and sitting in the clearance basket. It's chunky and wide, and it looks like it might fit me. I pick it up and try to slide my hand through. It will barely get past my knuckles. I try again, squeezing my fingers together as close as they can go, but the bracelet won't go on. I put it back into the basket.

"Excuse me," the salesclerk steps toward me. "I'm sorry. I just noticed you still have your bag with you. Do you mind if I take it and hold it behind the counter?"

"I, uh—"

"It's store policy."

I look around the store. The woman standing at the rack next to me has her clutch in her right hand. She is white. The woman two racks from her has a purse hanging on her left shoulder. Also white. Before I can object, she says, "Your bag is quite large. Much larger than theirs, which is why—"

"If you're not taking everyone's bag, you're not taking mine," I tell her.

"I'm sorry, but if you don't cooperate, I'll have to ask you to leave."

"Don't worry about asking me." I walk out of the store, right past all the other women who heard this lady ask me for my bag while they are still holding on to theirs. None of them say anything. Most look away, like they are trying not to witness this. Others stare and shake their heads in disappointment. I'm not sure if the gesture is geared toward me or the clerk.

I sit on a bench outside of the store and wait for Sam. One of the women who was able to hold on to her purse comes out of the store, a shopping bag in hand. She walks over to me and says, "I'm sorry to bother you, but I had to let you know that what that woman did to you was wrong. If I were you, I'd write a letter to her manager." She walks away, and I am left with her apology and the scent of her lingering perfume.

When Sam comes out, she asks, "Why'd you come out here?"

I tell her everything that happened.

"No way," she says.

"I'm serious. That really just happened," I tell her. "Did you get to take your backpack into the dressing room?"

She looks at mine, lifts it up to hers, and says, "Yes, but yours is a little bigger."

"By, what? An inch? Really, Sam? You're going to side with that racist salesclerk?"

We walk to the next store. "I wouldn't call that racist," Sam says.

"So what would you call it?"

"I don't know. Maybe you seemed up to something because you weren't buying any clothes."

"So big girls can't go into stores for skinny girls and look at the accessories? That's a problem too?"

Sam slows down. "That's not what I'm saying. I don't think it had anything to do with your race or your size. I think maybe she was just trying to do her job. That's all."

I don't know what's worse. Being mistreated because of the color of your skin, your size, or having to prove that it really happened.

35

negro
black

Today's collage is made up of words and cutouts from magazines.

Things That Are Black and Beautiful:

A Starless Night Sky
Storm Clouds
Onyx
Clarinets
Ink
Panthers
Black Swans
Afro Puffs
Michelle Obama

Me

36

comer

to eat

As soon as I step onto the porch, I can hear Fred Hammond's voice singing about God's grace and mercy. Mom must be home and she must be cooking or cleaning, because that's the only time she goes into gospel music mode. I unlock the door and walk in. "Mom!" I call out to make sure I don't scare her, since her back is to me.

She jumps anyway, all hysterical, but then smiles once she realizes it's just me. "Jade, you can't sneak up on me like that!"

I turn the music down. "Sorry. I tried not to."

Mom scratches her nose against her forearm because her hands are turning fish in a bowl of cornmeal, coating both sides before she dips it into hot oil in a frying pan. On the back burners of the stove, there are two silver pots, their lids trembling on top of them like chattering teeth. She turns the knobs down and brings the boiling pots to a simmer.

"You're home early," I say.

"Half day today."

I change my clothes, grab a bag of chips, and sit at the dining room table.

"Don't get full. Dinner will be ready soon." Mom takes the fish out of the frying pan and puts it on a plate layered with paper towels to soak up the grease. She puts more fish in the pan. The oil pops and crackles.

I eat a few more chips, fold the bag, and start doing my math homework. By problem three I am feeling stuck and frustrated. "I can't do this right now," I say. I close my book.

Mom comes over to me. "What's wrong?"

"Algebra two."

Mom opens my book, skims the page for a moment, and then says, "Girl, I don't know nothing 'bout that. Wish I could help you."

I close the book. "It's okay," I tell her. "I'll ask Maxine to help me."

"Well, excuse me," Mom says.

"Mom—"

"No, you're right. I can't help you. At all." Mom finishes cooking.

I take my flash cards out and drill myself. I repeat each word three times. Mom huffs and puffs and closes cabinets harder than usual, so I stop saying the words out loud. Just whisper them. Mom fixes my plate and then fixes hers.

I take a bite of the fish. "This is good, Mom." I tell her—not like she doesn't know it, but because I think she needs to be reminded of the good she can do. But if that was my goal, I should have stopped there. Because what I say next sends Mom into a rage. "Are you coming to the Woman to Woman Healthy Eating, Healthy Living seminar?"

"The what?"

"I left the flyer on the fridge." I point.

Mom looks at the flyer. "I don't have time to go to that. What is it about, anyway?"

"Eating healthy. I think they're going to give tips on how to make small changes when buying and cooking food. Like, this fish—it's good—so good, but Maxine and Sabrina would probably say it should be grilled or pan seared or—"

"Is Sabrina going to buy us a grill? You tell Maxine that if she got time to come over here and cook for us, she can come. Until then, I'm cooking how I want to cook." Mom shakes hot sauce onto her fish. "Got some nerve, telling me how to cook my food."

"That was only an example. I'm not—"

"I don't fry *everything*. Humph. You liked my cooking until you started going out with Maxine—"

"Mom, I love your cooking. I was just telling you about the event."

"You hanging around all those uppity black women who done forgot where they come from. Maxine know she knows about fried fish. I don't know one black person who hasn't been to a fish fry at least once in their life. Where she from?"

Mom won't stop talking. She goes on and on about Maxine and Sabrina and how they are a different type of black, how she knows she's going to get tired of dealing with them for the next two years. "I swear, if you didn't need that scholarship, I'd take you out of that program. I'm not sending you there to be in no cooking class. What that got to do with getting into college?"

I let Mom talk. I know none of these questions are meant to be answered. I finish eating, making sure I eat every single morsel of food on the plate.

37

mi madre
my mother

Photocopied pictures of my mother from when she was an infant till now are spread across the table. I rip and cut and puzzle her back together. The hair of her teen years; her hands, when she used to paint her nails, before they were constantly washing and scrubbing. The smile from her twenty-first birthday. The eyes she had when she was seven, before she really saw this world. All the best parts of her on the page.

38

vestido
dress

Mom and I stand at the fridge, looking at our dry-erase calendar. "Are you keeping up on your homework?" Mom asks. "All these activities can't get in the way of your studies."

"I know," I tell her. "I'm good."

She looks the calendar over, studying each date. She gets to next Friday and says, "Wow, the symphony? Woman to Woman sure does plan some extravagant events."

"I know. I can't wait. I've never been to a symphony before."

Mom says, "What are you going to wear? Don't people dress up to go to the symphony?"

"They do?" I ask.

"I think so. I guess you should ask Maxine. She should know."

Mom walks to her bedroom. I hear her mumble, "I've never been to the symphony either." Her door closes.

I go to my bedroom and stand in front of the closet, looking for something to wear. I try on at least five outfits. Nothing looks right. Either the shirt is too snug, the skirt too casual, the dress too dressy. I think about the money I put away just in case there was an emergency. A new dress isn't what I thought I'd use the money on, but I have to. I mean, after all, it's the symphony.

39

música
music

Before the symphony begins, one of the volunteers gives us a tour of the backstage area and talks about the history of the Oregon Symphony. She is white, and the black sweater she is wearing makes her skin look pale and washed-out. "You all should be very proud to be Oregonians. Did you know that before we were called the Oregon Symphony, we were called the Portland Symphony Society? We were the first orchestra in the West, and one of only seven major orchestras established in America before 1900." She seems very proud of this fact.

The volunteer walks us to the stage so we can see the same view the musicians will have tonight as they look out at the audience. She tells us, "I like to think of our musical sections as different families coming together for one big celebration. You see, instruments in certain families have things in common, like being made from the same types of material, looking similar, and sounding akin to each other. They come in all sizes, just like natural families have parents and children and extended family members."

I can tell this is something she's memorized. But still, she manages to say it to us with passion and a smile on her face.

She is hyper, talking fast and high-pitched like the chirping birds outside my window in the early morning. "Our families are the strings family, the woodwind family, the brass family, and the percussion family."

The volunteer must be offended that we aren't as excited as she is. Why else would she look at us and say, "You know, some folks don't think they can relate to this kind of music. But let me tell you, all kinds of people have been lovers of the symphony."

This part doesn't sound memorized. I think she's going off script.

"Now, I know hip-hop is what you kids are all about these days," she says. "But did you know that James DePreist was one of the first African American conductors on the world stage? In 1980 he became the music director of the Oregon Symphony, and he held the position for twenty-three years." She walks toward us a little, still smiling. "He truly transformed our little part-time orchestra to a nationally recognized company with several recordings." She pauses for a moment, maybe waiting for one of us to say something. Then she says, "Fun fact—he was the nephew of contralto Marian Anderson. Their family was from Philadelphia, but she lived in Portland in her last days. Do you know about her?"

Maxine speaks up. "Yes, we know about her." There is venom in her voice.

"Oh," the woman says with a smile.

Maxine is not smiling. She folds her arms and says, "In 1939, when she was refused permission to sing to an integrated audience in Constitution Hall, with the help of First Lady Eleanor Roosevelt, Marian Anderson performed a critically acclaimed concert on the steps of the Lincoln Memorial in Washington, DC. She traveled the world."

"Well, my, yes. That . . . that sums it up," the woman says.

"She was also the first black person to perform with the New York Metropolitan Opera," Maxine adds.

"Yes, well, looks like you know music history. I think that's great."

I hear Maxine's breathing intensify.

"Now," the volunteer says, "let's get you all to your seats."

We walk to our reserved seating and sit down, watching people file into the auditorium, dressed in their pearls and ties. Maxine whispers to Carla, "Can you believe that woman? Talking to us like we're some poor black heathens who don't know anything worth knowing."

Carla says, "I know, right? First of all, I don't even listen to hip-hop."

Listening to Maxine and Carla, I think maybe they aren't only offended at that woman's stereotypes, but maybe they are upset at the idea of being put in the same category as me and the other girls.

The lights fade.

My emotions are all mixed up and jumbled inside.

For the first two songs, all I can think about is that white woman's smiling face, her annoying voice. And even though we're all dressed up in our new clothes, even though none of us had opened our mouths and talked to her, she thought we were the kind of kids who wouldn't appreciate classical music. Makes me feel like no matter how dressed up we are, no matter how respectful we are, some people will only see what they want to see.

I try to let the music wash away that feeling that comes when white people make you feel special or stupid for no good reason. I don't know how to describe that feeling, just to say that it's kind of like cold, sunny days. Something is discomforting about a sun that gives no heat but keeps shining.

I close my eyes and try to listen to the music, really focus.

The melody is like an intricate collage. If you take it on all at once, you hear one song, one whole sound. But if you listen for the viola and cello, the flute and clarinet, you hear how each note lies next to the other to complete an image, how the French horn and tuba complements them all. How the piano and xylophone, the cymbals and drums hold them up like a base color. How the picture wouldn't be the same without each note in its just-right place.

I did not know about James DePreist, and I'd never heard of Marian Anderson. But tonight I feel myself dancing with them. Feel myself traveling the world.

40

el río
the river

The past few weeks have been slow and quiet. Mom is working extra shifts because she is determined to start saving money so she can put a down payment on a car. E.J. practically lives at the studio, so I am usually home by myself. Which is good. The house stays cleaner this way, and the food lasts longer.

I haven't spent much time with Sam. Partly because I usually have something to do after school, but mostly because I don't know how to be around her when I know she doesn't think that salesclerk treated me wrong. I don't even think she feels the tension between us. She has moved on and acts like everything is fine, but me? I'm stuck wondering if I can truly be friends with someone who doesn't understand what I go through, how I feel. I don't expect Sam to always agree with me, but she didn't even give me that generic *I'm sorry that happened to you* or *I'm sorry you feel that way* response.

Today, though, I have nowhere to go after school, so there is no avoiding Sam. She sees me at my locker as I swap out one book for another, and waits for me. "I have to stop by Mrs. Parker's office before I leave," she says.

"Okay."

We walk to Mrs. Parker's office, and when she sees us, she smiles and opens her jar. "What's your pleasure today?" she asks. She holds the jar out.

Sam takes two sour apple Jolly Ranchers. I take a cherry one.

Then Mrs. Parker says, "Jade, do you mind if I speak with Sam alone? Just for a moment."

"Oh, ah, okay. I'll wait out there, Sam." I point to the sitting area outside Mrs. Parker's office. I take one more Jolly Rancher and leave. When I step into the waiting area, I dump my bag onto one of the chairs and walk over to the alumni hall of fame wall. Here, the counselors have posted photos of graduates from last school year, each photo with a small sign under the name that lists the college the former graduates are attending. I smile, knowing my picture will be here one day.

Sam comes out of Mrs. Parker's office, an envelope in her hand and the biggest smile on her face. She can't even get words out, she is breathing and smiling so hard. "Oh my God, Jade. This is so unreal. You are not going to believe this!"

"What happened?"

We walk out of the counseling center and make our way to the bus stop. "I've been nominated for the study abroad program," she says. "This year the trip is to Costa Rica."

When she says this, there is a pain in my chest. A real physical pain. What I really want to do is turn around, go back to Mrs. Parker's office, and ask, *What about me?* Instead I say, "That's— Wow, Sam. That's— Congratulations." I feel horrible that I can't do better than that. I try again. "That's really amazing. What did Mrs. Parker say?"

"Well, she said I was nominated by Mr. Flores," Sam tells me. We get to the bus stop and wait. I can barely look at Sam right now, because I'm afraid she'll see my eyes and know how I really feel. I sit down and look out at the street. Sam opens her envelope. "There's an information session happening in two weeks. I have to bring an adult."

She keeps talking, but I lose track of what she is saying. I am too busy thinking, *How did this happen?* Too busy trying to concentrate on the moving cars and trucks so I can distract my tears from falling.

"What's wrong?" Sam asks.

If she has to ask, it's not worth explaining. "Nothing," I say. She probably wouldn't understand anyway.

"Are you sure?"

"Nothing's wrong."

The bus comes. We get on, show our bus passes, and head to our usual section. I get in first, sit next to the window. The bus jerks, and Sam stumbles into the seat next to me. Once she is situated in her seat, she turns to me and says, "You should come to the meeting too. The two of us in Costa Rica? That would be the best thing—"

"You have to be nominated to go, Sam. No one nominated me."

"But, well, maybe—"

"Maybe what?"

Sam puts the envelope into her backpack.

We ride in silence. Finally silence.

Passengers get on and off the bus. On and off.

Sam moves her too-long bangs out of her face. "What are you thinking about?"

"Nothing," I say.

"Are you mad at me?"

"No."

"Okay."

We're getting close to Sam's stop. She scoots forward, getting ready to get up even though there are at least four more blocks to go. Sam starts talking again. "I, uh, I was going to ask if you wanted to come over this weekend. Maybe spend the night?"

"I'll let you know what my mom says."

"We can make pizza. My grandpa taught me how to make it from scratch. You like pizza, right?"

I nod.

When the bus pulls over at Sam's stop, she walks to the back door. "See you tomorrow," she says.

"Bye."

I ride through the transition blocks, and then I'm back on my side of town. Where the river is polluted. I am thinking about the fish and the river. The giving and the learning. I am wondering how choices are made about who gets what and how much they get. Wondering who owns the river and the line, and the hook, and the worm.

41

familia
family

I haven't spent time with Maxine since the outing to the symphony. She's called a lot, but I usually make an excuse and say how busy I am and that I can't talk. But she was determined to hang out today, so she invited me to her family's Sunday dinner. "It's a tradition in my family to eat dinner together on the first Sunday of the month," Maxine tells me. "We call it Soul Food Sunday."

I am surprised when Maxine says this. She doesn't seem like the type of person who knows anything about soul food.

"I'm in charge of dessert," Maxine says. She studies the cakes inside the glass case. We're at some fancy bakery in the Pearl District, browsing through cakes, scones, and cookies. "What looks good to you?"

"Everything," I tell her.

She laughs. "Yeah, this is pastry heaven. I get myself in trouble when I come here on Fridays. Everything's half off on Fridays."

The baker behind the counter has just finished decorating a cake. She's sculpted it to look like a dollhouse. I doubt the little girl it's being made for will even want to cut into it. It looks so real. Too real to eat.

Maxine waves over one of the men behind the counter. "Can I get a dozen of these?" She points to the lemon-marionberry scones. Then she looks at me and says, "Now you pick something. A cake. Which one should we get?" She hands me the cake list.

I look it over: Sacher torte, pink champagne, crème de menthe, chocolate ganache. I go with the one that has chocolate in the name. You can't go wrong with chocolate.

"Good choice," Maxine says. "My dad loves chocolate ganache. You've won him over without even trying."

Maxine pays for the cake and scones, and we leave the bakery.

I can tell we're entering the rich part of Portland. We're driving up a winding road that's got us so high, my ears are popping. The road is secluded by tall trees tickling the sky. We come to a stop sign, and it feels like we might slide back down the hill. The car is at an angle, and I feel like I'm on a carnival ride that got stuck. Maxine looks both ways and begins to drive again. Then she says, "Look to your left."

I turn my head and see the city of Portland below, Mount Hood in the distance. Maxine makes a right turn onto a steep hill, leading us down into a cul-de-sac of houses. Wait, not houses. Mansions. I've seen places like this before, like when I watch those shows that give an inside look at celebrity homes. But I've never been inside one.

"We're here," Maxine says. She pulls up to a house that has three garage doors and a balcony that wraps around to the front of the house. The yard looks fake, too plush and green to be real.

A woman who looks just like Maxine is standing at the door. When we get out of the car, she calls out, "Max!"

"That's my sister, Mia," Maxine tells me.

They hug and we go inside.

It takes only seconds before Maxine's family is surrounding us, hugging us and welcoming me. Maxine introduces me to everyone: Maxine's brother, Nathan, and his wife, Abby, and Mr. and Mrs. Winters, Maxine's parents.

Nathan takes the cake out of my hand. It's clearly in a box that's labeled THE CAKE SHOP, but still he looks at his sister and says, "Oh no, you didn't bake this, did you, Max?"

Maxine hits him. "Not in front of company, please," she says.

He laughs, looks at me, and whispers, "At the last dinner she burned boiling water. Burned. Boiling. Water."

I try not to laugh too hard, but I can't help it.

Abby takes my jacket. Maxine lets me know that her mom prefers for people to take off their shoes. I take them off and add them to the row of shoes lined up against the wall. Everything in this house seems to have a place. No piles or messes. The walls look like curated museum exhibits. Maxine notices me looking at the art. "My mom loves collecting black art. It's all through the house. That's where Mia gets it from." Maxine calls out to her sister, "Mia, what's the name of this artist, again? The collection in the foyer?"

Mia yells, "Jacob Lawrence."

"Right," Maxine says. We walk into the kitchen.

Mia and Abby are putting food on serving dishes. I ask them if they need help with anything, but Mia insists that since I'm a guest, I should make myself comfortable.

I sit down on the small sofa—yes, a sofa in the kitchen, that's how big this place is—and watch the siblings orbit around one another, going back and forth between the stove, the fridge, the cabinets.

Mia says to me, "So tell us about yourself, Jade. You're an artist, right? I'd love to have you stop by my gallery."

"Thanks, I'd like that," I say.

Maxine says, "Yeah, I keep meaning to take you by there. I think you'll like it. And, Mia, you'll love Jade's work."

Mia and Abby switch off with the questions:

"What grade are you in?"

"Any siblings?"

"Do you like St. Francis?"

"What do you want to do after high school?"

Maxine interjects, "Don't bombard my mentee with questions," she says. "I've already told you, Jade is an artist and she's also a scholar." Maxine brags about me, telling them, "She's so focused. I just know she's going to be a successful woman one day."

Mia arranges crackers and cheese on a tray. She cuts the slices of cheese carefully. "And so you live in North Portland, right? Man, that's dedication—how early do you get up to get to school?"

"I get up at—"

"It's not that bad, is it, Jade?" Maxine asks. "You get up at, what? Six o'clock?"

"Are you going to let the girl speak?" Nathan says.

I was thinking the same thing.

Maxine is acting like she's afraid that if I open my mouth, I'll say the wrong thing, embarrass her or something. She seems nervous. I still don't get a word in because Mia says, "Well, I'll stop putting Jade on the spot. Let's talk about what our plans are going to be for summer vacation. I know it's a ways away, but we should at least start narrowing down a place," she says. She walks the tray into the dining room and sets it on a long table against the wall. The space is open, so even though she is in the dining room, I see her and the living room and even the staircase that must lead to the bedrooms all at once.

"I'm still on a high from our winter vacation," Abby says. "Sun Mountain Lodge was magnificent. Let's go there again." Abby is rinsing spinach so she can make the salad.

"I don't know," Mia says. "I was thinking we'd go someplace tropical. Sun Mountain Lodge won't be as fun without all the snow. The cross-country skiing was the best part."

Abby adds, "Let's not forget about that spa where we got the body and face treatment. I didn't want to leave." She places the spinach in the bowl and adds dried cranberries, goat cheese, and walnuts.

Nathan takes a piece of cheese out of the bowl. Abby slaps his hand. He takes another and says, "What about doing Victoria this summer?"

"Or northern California," Mia says.

The four of them move around, setting the table, making the final preparations to the food. They never decide on a place.

I wonder what it would be like to go on a family vacation. Mom and I have never traveled anywhere together. One day I'm going to take her somewhere. Somewhere far from Oregon. Someplace you have to get on a plane in order to get to.

Mr. and Mrs. Winters come back downstairs, and we all go into the dining room. The food on the table looks so elegant. Like a feast for a royal family, but it's really just baked macaroni and cheese, greens, candied yams, and ox tails with white rice. I wonder how it tastes, wonder if anything that looks this fancy can still taste how soul food is supposed to taste.

I sit down, Maxine beside me. She takes the folded linen napkin off her plate and drapes it on her lap, telling me with her eyes to do the same. I do.

After Mr. Winters prays over the food, I take the fork closest to my plate and begin to eat. Maxine gently taps me on my leg and whispers, "Wrong fork. Use the one farthest from the plate and work your way in throughout dinner."

I already have salad dressing on my fork and I know better than to lick it off and place the fork back on the table, so I just freeze.

"It's okay," Nathan says. He picks up the wrong fork too and starts eating. He winks at me and I keep eating, but for the rest of dinner, I am careful to watch what Maxine does.

The first bite of food is so good, I almost moan out loud. That's what we do at my house. The first five minutes is me and E.J. moaning and telling Mom, "Oh my goodness, this is so good," and "Mmm. Yes, yes." But I get the feeling that's not what Maxine's family does.

Once we're good into the meal, Mrs. Winters says, "So let's do our check-ins." She turns to her husband.

"Nothing new around here," he says. "I sold the house in Laurelhurst."

The room echoes with congratulations.

Mia is next. She finishes swallowing her food, takes a sip of her wine, and then says, "Work is amazing. I just put up a show of local emerging artists. We're getting lots of foot traffic." Mia takes another sip of her drink. "Tim and I are doing well. He sends his love. He really wanted to be here, but he's on call tonight and had to go in."

When she says this, Maxine whispers to me, "Her husband is a doctor."

Mia tosses a look to Nathan, who is sitting next to her. "And you?"

"All is well at the firm," Nathan says. "Work is work, you know. Same thing, different day." He puts his arm around his wife. "I'll let Abby tell you our real news."

Mrs. Winters puts her fork down. "I knew it! I knew it!"

Abby chuckles. "We don't know the sex yet. The sonogram is next week," she says.

Mrs. Winters gets out of her seat and hugs Abby, squeezing her tight. Mr. Winters pats Nathan on his back. "Congratulations, son. My boy, a father." He shakes his head.

I look at Maxine, who is the only one not smiling. She rakes her yams from one side of the plate to the other, never taking a bite. Once she sees me staring at her, she snaps out of it, smiles, and gets up to hug Abby. "I can't believe I'm going to be an auntie," she says. "I'm going to be the baby's favorite. Just saying."

Everyone is so excited about Nathan's announcement that the family check-in stops, and all Mrs. Winters can do is make plans for the baby shower. No one asks Maxine if she has any news. I can tell Maxine is hurt by this. Because when Mia says, "We should paint a mural in the baby's nursery. That would be so much fun, wouldn't it, Maxine?" Maxine says, "Yeah, sure. That would be awesome," but her voice is flat and without emotion.

Mrs. Winters brings out dessert. I am still eating, but I notice that everyone else has left a little bit on their plates, so I do too. In my house, there is no wasting food. Not one morsel of it. But here, I think it's some way of showing you don't eat too much, that you are saving room for dessert.

Everyone gawks over how beautiful the cake is. "Jade picked it," Maxine says.

Mr. Winters looks at me. "Great choice," he says.

We eat dessert—the best cake I've ever had—and then Mrs. Winters pushes her chair back from the table. "Jade, honey, would you please rescue my family from these calories and take some of this food home?"

"Oh, that's okay. No, I—I don't want to take your—"

"I insist," she says.

She smiles and gets up from the table and goes into the kitchen. "Come."

I follow her.

Mrs. Winters makes five Tupperware containers for me. And there's food wrapped in foil, and a bottle of sparkling cider. She places the food in a canvas tote bag. Then she cuts a few slices of cake. "My husband will finish this off tonight if you don't take some," she says. She wraps the slices of cake individually.

Maxine comes into the kitchen. She sees the stuffed bag and says, "Mom, there are only three people who live there. I think that's good."

"Well, this way they can have seconds," Mrs. Winters says. "Would you like me to make you a to-go plate too, Max?" She says this with less generosity in her voice.

"No, thank you."

"You sure? I'm only trying to help. Not like you're working or anything—"

"Mom. I said no, thank you."

I walk over to the sofa and sit down. I know it isn't like I can't still hear them, but for some reason it feels better to be over here instead of in the middle of them.

"Well, honey, now don't get upset. You know I worry about you. It's very *nice* what you're doing with Jade," she says.

Maxine whispers—kind of. Her voice is low, but I am close enough that I still hear her. "Mom, it's not just *nice* what I'm doing with Jade. Woman to Woman is making a difference in her life. I was hoping that by bringing her here, you'd see I am doing something that matters." Then she lowers her voice even more and walks farther away from me.

I can't hear what she says, but Mrs. Winters's voice is loud and clear. "I don't care about her sob story, Max. I understand that program is important to you, but you need a real job. Your father and I can't keep—"

Nathan walks in, carrying a handful of dishes. He rakes the remnants of dinner into the trash and hands the plates to Abby so she can load the dishwasher. Maxine and Mrs. Winters stop talking, and I am so glad. I don't want to hear any more about Mrs. Winters's resentment toward her daughter for being my mentor. I want to leave. Just want to go back to my mother and eat the food at her table that has no rules about the way to use forks and napkins. Want to go where I don't have to pretend I'm not hungry, where I can eat all that's on my plate and not feel greedy.

I do not want to be Maxine's experiment, charity case, or rebellious backlash against her mother. I do not want her to feel she has to coach me on what to say.

We say good-bye to everyone and leave.

Maxine and I ride down the hill. The sky is dark now, and the road is slick with rain. The side-to-side, side-to-side rhythm of the windshield wipers fills the silence. In the dark these majestic houses feel creepy, hidden away in all the trees and tucked behind alcoves. When we get to the bottom of the hill, Maxine says, "I'm not sure what you heard."

"Please don't. Just— Let's not talk. Please take me home." I don't want an explanation or an apology. That feeling comes again, tightness in chest, tears in eyes. My mouth on lockdown, no words coming out. But they are there; I feel them rising.

42

saber
to know

Mom knows the food in the fridge is from Maxine's mom. The ticket stub from Portland Art Museum and the program from the Artists Repertory Theatre are both outings Woman to Woman arranged.

Mom knows.

She is sleeping to work, and working to eat, and working, and working, and working,

And Mom knows that when she asks me, "How was your day?"

And I say, "It was fine," that I am leaving out the details to spare her from hearing how the village is raising her child.

"So, things are going well with this mentoring thing, huh?" Mom presses. "And to think, you didn't even want to give Maxine a chance." Mom eats another forkful of Mrs. Winters's food. "Now you're with her all the time. Just loving it, huh?"

"I wouldn't say I love it," I tell her. "I'm actually thinking about quitting."

Mom puts her fork down. "What happened?"

"Nothing."

"Jade, nothing happened but you want to quit? Come on, now."

"I'm serious. Nothing happened. Nothing's happening. That's the problem. I just . . . I don't know. I feel like half the time I'm Maxine's charity case—"

"That's it? That's why you want to quit?" she asks. "Look, Jade. You are not quitting that program. Who do you think is going to pay for you to go to college? Not me, no matter how much I save. Not your daddy—"

"Mom, I can find another way to get a scholarship," I tell her. "I have good grades and I'm sure I'll get a decent SAT score—"

"This isn't *only* about a scholarship!"

"It isn't?" I say.

"Don't get smart with me. First of all, I didn't raise you to be a person who walks away from commitments. Someone else could have taken your spot. Second of all, not every girl has a young woman like Maxine to look up to. You need to learn that burning bridges always has a consequence."

"But I don't look up to Maxine," I tell her. "She's using me to feel better about herself. And her mother gave us all this food because she feels sorry for us. If that's how you act when you have money, I'd rather stay poor."

Poor. I actually said the word out loud. To my mom. About us.

"That's a foolish thing to say, Jade." Mom gets up and walks to her bedroom. "A very foolish thing to say." When Mom comes back to the kitchen, she is carrying a jar of coins. A big jar, like maybe she bought something at Costco and saved the container. "You want this to be your life, Jade?" Mom sets the jar in the middle of table. "You want to grow up and have children and only have this to leave behind as an inheritance?"

Mom is talking to me in her I'm-so-mad-at-you-I-can't-even-yell-at-you voice. I really wish she would just yell at me.

"Now let me be clear: having money doesn't make you successful. I know that. And I'm not saying Maxine is perfect, but I am saying that even imperfect people have things to teach you," Mom says. "You're too smart to be acting so stupid, Jade. You see how hard I'm working, trying to save every extra penny I get so you can have some kind of life, and you just going to throw away an opportunity that'll get you into college? So what, Maxine isn't perfect? This girl graduated from St. Francis as valedictorian. She learned how to navigate this white world, and she is trying to show you how to do the same. You telling me she has nothing to teach you? You better learn how to get from this opportunity what you can and let the rest fall off your back," Mom says. "You understand what I'm saying, Jade?"

I sit still and listen. I know better than to talk back and start an argument.

"You better figure out a way to stay in this program and finish strong. You hear me? Figure it out."

43

tener dolor
to have pain

Today we learn words that pertain to going to the doctor. Mr. Flores is always teaching about one kind of thing while I'm thinking about another.

No me siento bien. I don't feel well.

Tengo dolor. I have pain.

Me duele aquí. It hurts here.

44

hablar
to speak

I miss the next two outings with Maxine. I lied and told her I had too much homework so Mom wouldn't let me go. I lied and told Mom the outings were canceled. I don't even miss them. I mean, I miss the free food and I miss going to places I probably would have never gone to on my own. But I don't miss the lectures about how to eat, how to not be who I am.

I am lying in my bed, thinking about all this and looking around my room, at the walls, at the ceiling. There's a crack in the wall I've never noticed until now, and a spider is building her web in the corner of the ceiling. The wind is blowing and beating against my window; the rattling sounds like a nervous drum. The rain sounds like a million hands clapping in a stadium. Every now and then a car passes, speeding down the street on its way to somewhere. I hear the pipes moan when E.J. turns on the water in the kitchen. I hear the doorbell ring, then his footsteps into the living room, then Lee Lee's voice. Before I can sit up, she is knocking on my door. "Come in," I tell her. I don't care that I am not dressed, that my hair is pulled back in a sloppy bun.

When Lee Lee comes in, the first thing she says is, "What's the matter with you?" She sits on the foot of my bed and stares me down with her you-better-not-lie-to-me look.

"Nothing," I tell her. "Tired."

"Why does your mom think I need to talk to you?"

"Are you serious? She sent you over here?"

"No. I was already on my way. We passed each other while she was going to work. She said maybe I can talk some sense into you. But didn't give me details. What's going on?"

"Nothing."

"Jade—"

"I'm *thinking* about quitting Woman to Woman."

"But don't you get a scholarship for being in that program?"

I sigh. "I am so tired of talking about it."

"Well, you haven't talked about it with me," Lee Lee says.

I don't say anything.

"Look, I don't know what's going on with you, but I know you are too smart to give up on yourself."

"I'm not giving up on myself."

"Yes, you are. Whatever happened, it's not worth quitting. Who loses if you quit the program? Not Maxine. You do.

You're the one who'll be trying to figure out how to pay back a school loan."

"But you don't understand," I tell Lee Lee. "I don't want to go to all these expensive restaurants and be reminded that my family can't afford to eat in them. I don't want be taken all over the city of Portland just so I can see how everyone else lives in bigger and better houses and neighborhoods. I wanted to be in Woman to Woman because I thought I'd actually learn something about being a woman. About how to be a successful woman. So far all I've learned is how to make sure there are low-fat, vegan-friendly snacks at girl talk sessions. It's got me thinking, is that all mentorship is? Taking someone younger than you to places they can't afford?"

By the look on Lee Lee's face, she doesn't think any of these are good reasons to quit. I even tell her how sometimes Maxine makes me feel like I am better than my friends at Northside, better than Lee Lee. I add that part to get her on my side.

But instead Lee Lee says, "You need to talk to whoever is in charge. Have you said anything to anyone?"

I don't answer.

"They can't read your mind. I mean, I get what you're saying—some of that stuff is a little corny, and a lot of it is offensive. But I don't know; what's the better option? Stay silent, leave the program, and they never have a chance to do better?"

"But I could speak up and they could dismiss me. I mean, I doubt they'll take me seriously. They'll probably just make excuses," I tell her. "And I shouldn't have to tell grown people how to act. This is *their* program."

"It's their program, but it's for *you*," she says. "If you speak up and they dismiss you, that's on them. But if you stay quiet and just quit, well—"

"All right, all right. I'll think about it," I tell Lee Lee. I don't know why I never considered it before. Here I am, so focused on learning to speak another language, and I barely use the words I already know.

I need to speak up for myself. For what I need, for what I want.

Like most times, Lee Lee is right. I love and hate that about her.

45

la verdad
the truth

The next day, I call Maxine and ask if we can get together. She says yes right away, and we make plans for Saturday afternoon. When she gets to my house, she steps inside and brings the cold in with her. "Jade!" Maxine reaches out to hug me. "I missed you." Her hug is tight and long. "It is so good to see you." She holds on to me as if to say, *I'm sorry for hurting you.* As if to say, *I'm not going to stop calling or coming by; I'm committed to you.* "Ready?" she asks.

"Ready." We get into her car. It's beginning to sprinkle, so Maxine turns the wipers on the lowest speed and I watch the water disappear and come back again. Sabrina is always telling us girls that we need to work on making eye contact with people. That people want to know we're telling the truth and that we're confident and sure of ourselves. But I feel more confident when I'm looking at the floor or my shoes or far away at the rain clouds. I know I don't have a choice, so like my mom and Lee Lee keep telling me, I start speaking. "I'm sorry I've been flaking out on you."

"Do you want to tell me what's going on?"

"I want something more from Woman to Woman," I tell her. "I don't want to sound ungrateful. I mean, I do like going on all those trips, but sometimes you make me feel like you've come to fix me; only, I don't feel broken. Not until I'm around you."

Maxine doesn't say anything. She keeps driving, keeps listening.

"It feels like Woman to Woman takes us to all these places outside of our neighborhood, as if the places in our neighborhood aren't good enough." I pause to see if she's going to say anything. She doesn't. So I keep going. I say it all, "When you invited me over to have dinner with your family, I thought that was so nice of you. I thought you wanted to spend time with me and get to know me and that you cared about me enough to meet your family. But it felt like you just wanted to use me to get at your mom and prove some kind of point to her. Like you were showing off. You didn't even let me speak for myself. I get so confused—because some of the time you act like you're proud of me, and other times you act like you're ashamed."

Maxine pulls into the parking lot of McMenamins on Thirty-Third. She takes her seat belt off, but we don't get out right away.

"Jade, I'm sorry. I feel horrible that you've been holding on to all of this," Maxine says. "I've got a lot of learning to do. I'm so sorry I hurt you in the process." Maxine sounds like she is about to cry, but the tears don't fall. "I don't pity you, Jade. Not at all. I don't pity your friends. And you're right: I shouldn't be speaking for you. Ever. Sometimes I overcompensate, I think. I want to make sure you are comfortable, that you don't feel on the spot—and well, I am proud of you, so maybe I brag a bit, make sure people know you are not the statistic they may be assuming you are. But yeah, you have a mouth and you can say all these things yourself."

This conversation isn't as intense as I thought it would be.

Maxine asks, "So what are some things Woman to Woman can do better?"

I take my seat belt off. "Well, I'd like to learn about real-life things—I mean, like you know, how to create a budget and balance a checkbook so I'll know how much money I can spend and how much to put aside so the lights don't get turned off," I tell her. "You know, stuff like that. I do like a lot about the program. I'm not saying we should stop those outings, but it just seems like we can do more."

"Jade, I don't feel that you're unappreciative. I think you're right. We could do better," Maxine says. "Any other ideas you have?"

"I've been thinking, what if we do a visit to your sister's gallery? Maybe she can talk about how she started her own business."

"Let's talk to Sabrina. I'm sure she'll think it's a great idea."

Maxine reaches to the backseat and grabs her purse. Before she opens the door, she asks, "Anything else you want to talk about?"

I didn't think I would say it, but when I open my mouth, "Jon," comes out. "It's kind of hard to believe you care about me when you're always standing me up for him," I tell her.

Maxine sighs a slow deep breath. "You're right," she says. She opens the door. "Let's talk about him over dinner."

46

abandonar
to quit

As we walk through McMenamins, Maxine acts like a tour guide. "Isn't it cool that this used to be a school? I love how they renovate old buildings. You know, they've done a funeral home, too."

"I'd never want to go there. Ever."

Maxine laughs. "There's one close to your house, but this one is my favorite," she tells me. We walk down a hall, and Maxine shows me what used to be the boiler room. It's a bar now. "You're too young to go in there. But maybe I'll take you on your twenty-first birthday." Maxine smiles at me.

I smile too and wonder if I'll know her past high school.

"Here's the movie theater," Maxine says. "I love coming here. All the seats are secondhand couches and chairs. You can bring food from the restaurant in there too," she says. "It's a perfect cheap place for a date."

"You sound like you work here or something."

"Just come here a lot," Maxine says.

We walk into the restaurant and wait to be seated. There are all kinds of lights hanging from the ceiling that are different sizes, shapes, and colors. They're kind of weird looking, but also beautiful.

The hostess seats us at the window that overlooks the patio, which has a garden and outdoor fireplace. Maxine takes the lemon wedge that's on the rim of her glass, squirts it into her water, and takes a sip. "So after meeting Kira and Bailey, I'm sure you see that you are not the first person to be anti-Jon," she says.

"I don't think we're anti-Jon. I think we're pro-Maxine," I say.

Maxine smiles as tears fall. She wipes them quickly. "Oh, Jade, you have me in here, getting all emotional. You're not supposed to be giving me the advice," she says.

Now that I've spoken honestly with Maxine and she's really listened, I feel like I can tell her anything. "I know I am the mentee," I say. "But for what it's worth, I don't think he deserves your time or any more attention from you."

Maxine says, "I know." Then: "I need to be better at setting boundaries and letting go." She takes in a deep breath, releases it real slow, and puts her mentor voice back on. "And you need to work on not giving up so easily. How about we make a deal? I quit Jon; you don't quit the program."

"Deal."

47

orar

to pray

If I don't leave in the next ten minutes, I'm going to be late for school. I put two Pop-Tarts into the toaster and don't even wait for them to shoot up. I slide the warm pastries back into the silver sleeve and put them into my backpack. I'll eat them on the bus. I walk into the living room. E.J. is awake but still lying down, looking at his phone. "Morning," he mumbles.

"Good morning." I put my coat on and zip it.

"You hear about what happened Saturday night?" E.J. asks.

"No."

He sits up and reads from his phone, "'Vancouver, Washington, police manhandle black teen at house party.'"

"What?" Vancouver is just across the Columbia River. It's practically in my backyard—just a fifteen-minute drive from my house. Most of the black people I know who live there used to live in Portland. "What's her name?" I ask.

E.J. looks at his phone, scrolling up and down with his finger. "Natasha Ramsey," he says. "She's fifteen." He turns the phone to me so I can see the photo.

I don't recognize her name or face, but still, she looks familiar. Like a girl I would be friends with. "What . . . what happened?"

"The police beat her bad. She's in critical condition." E.J. reads the article, calling out details as he reads. "The police were called to a house party because neighbors complained about loud music. The cops are saying when they came to break up the party, she was insubordinate." He reads for a few moments, than tells me, "They are saying they didn't use excessive force. But this girl has fractured ribs and a broken jaw!" E.J. shakes his head and puts down the phone. "We probably wouldn't even know about this except people had their phones out, recording."

"I feel like we should say a prayer or something."

"Why?"

"For Natasha Ramsey. For her family."

"And what is prayer going to do?" E.J. asks. "Prayer ain't nothing but the poor man's drug."

"What?"

"Poor people are the ones who pray. People who don't have what they need, who can't pay their rent, who can't buy healthy food, who can't save any of their paycheck because every dollar is already accounted for. Those are the people who pray. They pray for miracles, they pray for signs, they pray for good health.

Rich people don't do that," he tells me. "Plus, God isn't the one we need to be talking to. We need to talk to the chief of police, the mayor, and the governor. They're the ones with the power to make change."

I stare at the picture, can't stop looking at her face, at how she looks like someone who lives in my neighborhood. Maybe she used to? I see the time at the top of the screen. "I'm going to be late!" I yell. I've definitely missed the bus.

I rush to the door, but before I leave, E.J. stops me. "Be careful today, Jade. For real."

"I will."

When I get to school, the tardy bell for first period is ringing. I go to class, and the entire time all I can think about is Natasha Ramsey. Her smiling face. The bell rings, and I go to my locker. Sam is waiting for me. "Thought maybe you were sick and weren't coming today," she says.

"Nope, just couldn't get out the house on time today." I almost ask Sam if she heard about Natasha Ramsey, but I figure since she didn't say anything about it, she probably hasn't. I go to my next class, saying a prayer in my head as I walk down the hall.

48

fantasma
ghost

It is lunchtime. Sam and I are in the cafeteria, standing in line to fix our burrito bowls. All day long I've been whispering prayers. Natasha's name haunts me. No one speaks her name or mentions what happened. It's as if no one in this school knows or cares that an unarmed black girl was assaulted by the police just across the river.

My stomach hurts. And all I want to do is talk to my mom and Lee Lee and Maxine. Every time something like this happens, I go to accounting for every person I know who also fits the description, who it could've been. Feels like such a selfish thing to do—to be thankful it isn't someone I know. To call people just to hear their breath on the other end of the line.

"Excuse me, young lady. I'm not going to tell you again. Keep the line moving. Step up, step up." The voice interrupts my thoughts, and I realize Ms. Weber is talking to me. She is a short woman with hair to her waist. We've exchanged hellos every now and then but we've never had a conversation. "You too, Hannah," she says to the white girl in back of me. Sam is in front of us and has already put her rice and black beans in the bowl.

"God, Ms. Weber, don't have a heart attack about it," Hannah says.

I turn to Hannah and say, "I know, right? Is it that serious?" I pick up my bowl and get ready to dish my rice.

Ms. Weber stands in front of me. "You have a problem, young lady?"

"My name is Jade," I tell her.

"I didn't ask you what your name was. I asked you if you had a problem."

I roll my eyes. "You so worried about the line moving and now you're holding us up," I say. I try to pass her, but she won't move.

"You need to adjust your attitude," Ms. Weber says.

I walk around Ms. Weber. I put a scoop of rice and beans in my bowl.

Hannah is behind me. She laughs. "What is your problem today, Weber? PMS? Didn't get laid last night? I mean, God, what is it?"

I laugh, and as I put my grilled chicken in the bowl, Ms. Weber says, "Okay, that's it. Go see Mrs. Parker."

I don't think she's talking to me, so I keep moving down the line. Sam is finished making her lunch and has gone to find us a seat.

"Did you hear me, young lady? Go see Mrs. Parker. Now."

"My name is Jade, and why do I have to go see Mrs. Parker?"

"Because she's the only one in this school who can handle you. Come with me," she says.

She snatches my lunch out of my hands, throws it into the trash can, and escorts me out of the cafeteria. When we get to Mrs. Parker's office, Ms. Weber says, "Shirley, I need to speak with you." Then she turns to me and says, "You can stay here."

I stand against the wall. Mrs. Parker doesn't close her door, so I'm not sure what the point is of having me stand out here. I hear everything Ms. Weber is saying, every lie and exaggeration. "This girl needs to lose her attitude. I am not going to tolerate all that sass. She was so disrespectful, Shirley."

I get up and walk toward them. "Did you tell her what you said? Did you tell her that Hannah was being disrespectful too?"

Mrs. Parker turns to me. "Jade, please wait for me. I'll come out and hear your side too."

"I'm not going to let her lie on me, Mrs. Parker. I didn't do anything—"

"See what I mean?" Ms. Weber says. "Young lady, your defiant behavior can get you kicked out of this school."

"Let's all calm down," Mrs. Parker says.

Now there's a scene. Other counselors and students who are in the counseling center are staring. I refuse to put on a show for them. I stop talking. Stand back against the wall and wait. By the time Mrs. Parker is ready for me, lunch is over. She calls me into her office and sits across from me, behind her desk. "Are you okay to stay at school today or do you need to go home?"

"Mrs. Parker, I didn't do anything—"

"Jade, lower your voice. I'm only asking you a question. I'm trying to help you. If you need to take a moment and clear your head for the day, you can go home. But if you choose to stay, you'll have to let go of the attitude and—"

"I want to go home," I tell her. *And I never want to come back to this school again.*

"I think that's a good choice," Mrs. Parker says. "We'll start fresh tomorrow."

"I thought you wanted to hear my side," I say. "I didn't do anything, Mrs. Parker."

"Look, Jade, you're not in trouble."

"So you know Ms. Weber is lying?"

"I know both of you probably let this go too far and that it's a good idea to simply move on from this misunderstanding."

I bite my lip, hold back the tears that are boiling in my eyes. I think about Lee Lee and Maxine and how they're always telling me to speak up for myself. But right now I can't talk. Nothing but curse words would come out, anyway. So I stay silent.

I walk out of her office and go to my locker. Before I leave, I stop by Mr. Flores's class. He has a prep period after lunch, so I know he won't have students in his class. His door is open. He's reading something on his lap top and eating a sandwich. "Mr. Flores?"

"Yes?"

"I'm going home early today, and I just wanted to know if you can tell me what the homework is going to be."

"Well, sure, but is everything okay?"

"I'm fine," I tell him. If I talk about it, these tears will spill over.

Mr. Flores talks me through today's lesson and gives me the homework. "If you have questions, you can stop by at lunch tomorrow."

"Okay. Thanks." I look down at Mr. Flores's computer. The screen has a photo of Natasha Ramsey on it, next to an article. "Bye, Mr. Flores."

"Bye, Jade. Hope you feel better."

49

el teléfono
the telephone

"Are you okay?" Sam asks. She sounds like maybe she's washing dishes. "I can't believe they sent you home."

"I know. I didn't even do anything," I say.

"Well, you were mouthing off, Jade. I mean, I could never talk to a teacher like that."

"Yes, you could. Hannah did."

The water shuts off. I hear dishes clank, then a drawer open and close. "Well, you know why Hannah didn't get in trouble," Sam says.

"Because she's white."

I can't see Sam, but I'm pretty sure she just rolled her eyes. "Uh, no. Because she's rich. Her parents donate a bunch of money to the school every year. She can say and do whatever she

189

wants," Sam says. "That had nothing to do with her being white and your being black."

"You know that's what people are going to say about Natasha Ramsey. That it had nothing to do with her being black."

"Who?" Sam asks.

There is silence between us.

I don't respond, because this is not a conversation I want to have. Not with Sam. I tell her I have to go, that my mom needs the phone. I hang up. Call Lee Lee.

50

respirar
to breathe

The first thing Lee Lee says to me is, "I was just about to call you. Did you hear what happened?"

"Yeah. I've been thinking about it all day."

"We had a town hall meeting for students who needed to talk about it. I went," Lee Lee tells me.

"Did you say anything?" I ask.

"No, just listened. It was kind of pointless. I mean, you know, the usual, 'If you need an adult to talk to, we're here for you.' You know, that kind of stuff."

"Well, that's more than my school," I tell her.

"I want to do something," Lee Lee says.

"Do something?"

"Yeah, I mean, well, I kind of am, I guess. Mrs. Baker gave us an assignment to write a poem in honor of Natasha Ramsey or any victim of police brutality. But writing a poem doesn't seem like enough. I don't know." Lee Lee's voice cracks, and she stops talking. I hear her sniffing and breathing hard.

I get up off my bed and walk around my room. "You okay?"

"I don't know why this making me so, so . . . I don't know. I mean, we hear about this stuff all the time—and she didn't even die. It's not even as bad as it could be. But for some reason I just . . . I don't know. I feel, it just feels—"

"Too close?"

"Yeah, I guess."

"And like it could have been you or me?"

There are no words from Lee Lee, only the sound of her breathing.

We sit there, not talking, just listening to each other's breath. Just thankful.

51

borrar

to erase

Morning will be here soon and I haven't slept at all.

How does time go by without you seeing it, hearing it, feeling it? Have I yawned? Did my stomach moan? Did my eyes fade at least once?

I decide to make another piece about York.

In Clark's journals, he wrote that many Native Americans were fascinated with York's dark skin, his hair, his big frame. I can just hear them asking,

What are you?

Where are you from?

Why are you so dark?

What happened to you?

Clark wrote that some of the tribes thought York was magic, thought he was some kind of supernatural being. York would tell them he was a black man, nothing had happened to his skin, he was not a supernatural being. But some of them didn't believe him. So he joked around with the children, telling them monstrous tales, making himself into an evil, scary being. The children loved to laugh and run away from him.

I wonder how he felt at night. When the star-filled sky blanketed him, did he ever think about what his life was like before the expedition? Before he was a slave? How far back could he remember? Did he remember existing in a world where no one thought him strange, thought him a beast?

Did he remember being human?

52

perseverar
to persevere

Maxine and I decide to go on a walk through Columbia Park. "All our outings can't be centered around food," she says. Spring is finally here, so walking outside isn't so bad. I've been looking forward to it all week. We walk under the colossal trees, circling the whole park. As we walk, I tell her about Sam— about the incident at the mall and in the cafeteria line, and how Sam doesn't even know about Natasha Ramsey. How she's always making excuses for why something is the way it is, and her reasons are never about the fact that I am black and that sometimes it really is about race.

"You need to tell her how you feel," Maxine says.

"I know, but I don't know how to start the conversation with her," I admit. "And I've never had to have any serious conversations about race with a friend. I mean, the point of friendship is to be able to be yourself, to just exist with someone who gets you while you get them. I never have to talk to Lee Lee and hash things out about stuff like this."

"I don't think it's fair to compare the two of them. They are different, and just like Lee Lee offers you a certain kind of friendship, it sounds like Sam does too. Some friends are worth fighting for," Maxine says. She sits on a park bench. I sit next to her. "And you know, *you're* worth fighting for," Maxine tells me. "Did you ever talk with Mrs. Parker about the study abroad program?"

Something else I need to speak up about.

"I will," I tell her.

"By the way," she says. "I've been thinking of our deal. I held up my part," she tells me. "I'm done with Jon. For real this time. Thought you'd want to know that," Maxine says. "So, I did my part. I quit. Now we have to keep working on your learning how not to quit on everything and everyone because they disappoint you or hurt you or make a mistake."

I don't even argue with her because I know she's right. I can't quit on Sam, can't quit on my dream to do the study abroad program. Can't quit on me.

53

para abogar
to advocate

When I walk into the classroom, Mr. Flores is eating lunch and watching a video on his lap top. I hear a voice saying, *"Natasha Ramsey was released from the hospital this morning."*

Mr. Flores pauses the video. "Sorry, I forgot we had an appointment." He pushes his sandwich to the side. "Come on over, Jade. Have a seat."

"You can finish watching that, if you want," I tell him.

"Oh, this? I was watching the press conference they had this morning on Natasha Ramsey's case. But I can get to it later," he says.

"I'd like to watch it with you, if that's okay." I sit at Mr. Flores's desk. He touches the play button. We watch the doctor finish his statement, and then Vancouver's mayor speaks. Someone representing the family ends by thanking the citizens of the Vancouver-Portland area for their support and prayers.

When the video is over, Mr. Flores says, "I'm so relieved she's going to be okay. Physically, anyway. Who knows what the psychological damage will be?" He closes his computer. "Thanks for suggesting we watch it together," he says. "So, ah, ¿qué pasa?"

I hesitate. My problem seems trivial now after remembering Natasha Ramsey. There are worse things happening in this world. But if I don't say it now, I never will. "I just wanted to ask a question," I say. "I— I wanted to know why you didn't think to nominate me for the study abroad program." I look away, down at the floor, before I get a glimpse of his reaction.

"Well, Jade, that's a good question."

I give him my reasons why I think I deserve to go. "I have an A in your class. You always pick me to help people in the class who are struggling. And, you know, this is an opportunity to do volunteer work and service and that would look really good on my college résumé; plus, without the study abroad program, I doubt I'll ever, ever get an opportunity to travel internationally." Maybe I shouldn't have said that last point, but it's true. And he needs to know.

Mr. Flores's face changes color like a mood ring. He is white, pink, red. He takes a deep breath. "You are right that, technically, you deserved to go, but, well, I wanted to be fair to the other students," he tells me. "You have a lot of support and are in a lot of programs." He pauses, then continues, "Jade, other students need opportunities too." Then he wraps up the rest of his sandwich and puts it back into his bag.

"I'm not saying the students who were nominated shouldn't have been. I'm saying I should have been too. Why am I only seen as someone who needs and not someone who can give?" I ask.

Mr. Flores doesn't answer my question. Instead he says, "Don't you realize you're in those programs because we believe in you? We know you have potential. That SAT prep class you were in last year is going to make it easier for you when it comes time to take the test." Mr. Flores sits forward in his seat, like he's going to stand, like he's ready to go and be done with this conversation.

I get up.

Mr. Flores stands, walks me to the door. "It's my job to care about all my students, Jade. I have to be fair," he tells me.

Fair? I can't leave without telling him the rest of how I feel. I turn to him and make sure I am not raising my voice or talking with any attitude. It's a sincere question. "How is it fair that the girl who tutors half the people chosen for the study abroad trip doesn't get to go? You've given me an A plus every semester. Every semester. And you didn't think it would be fair to nominate me?" I didn't expect for the tears to come. First they are in my throat. My voice is weak, shaking. And I realize I am not just mad about all of this. I am sad. I face the door before any tears fall. "You don't have to answer that," I tell him. "Thanks for letting me talk with you." I leave the room while I still have control over my emotions. I hear Mr. Flores say something. Maybe, "I'm sorry." Maybe just, "Good-bye."

I go into the bathroom, hide away in the stall, and let out everything I was holding in. I hear footsteps and flushes and running water, and I wait until I know for sure no one is here before I step out.

I doubt my conversation with Mr. Flores will change anything. But at least he knows how I feel. At least I spoke up.

54

la primavera
spring

Sometimes I just want to be comfortable in this skin, this body. Want to cock my head back and laugh loud and free, all my teeth showing, and not be told I'm too rowdy, too ghetto. Sometimes I just want to go to school, wearing my hair big like cumulous clouds without getting any special attention, without having to explain why it looks different from the day before. Why it might look different tomorrow. Sometimes I just want to let my tongue speak the way it pleases, let it be untamed and not bound by rules. Want to talk without watchful ears listening to judge me. At school I turn on a switch, make sure nothing about me is too black. All day I am on. And that's why sometimes after school, I don't want to talk to Sam or go to her house, because her house is a reminder of how black I am.

It's the weekend before spring break. I promised to go over to sit with Sam while she packs for her trip to Costa Rica. She leaves tomorrow. Right now she is in the attic, getting a suitcase. I am in the living room with her grandfather. "So, what do you think of the Natasha Ramsey incident?" he asks.

I am not sure how to answer his question, because nothing but pain will pour out. I tell him, "I'm really sad about it." I tell him *sad* because I think white people can handle black sadness better than black anger. I feel both. But sadness gets sympathy, so I stick with that.

"It's really a shame," Mr. Franklin says. "If you ask me, I think all cops need training on race relations. That girl was just being a teenager, and teenagers shouldn't be brutalized for acting their age."

When he says this, the tension in my chest dissolves.

"I don't know what it's going to take for this country to live up to its promise," Mr. Franklin says. He shakes his head and sighs a deep sigh.

Sam comes back from the attic, and I am eager to go to her room, to talk about anything other than Natasha Ramsey. "Sorry it took so long," she tells me.

We walk into her room. The floor is covered with jeans, shirts, belts, and sweaters. "I don't have any summer clothes to bring," Sam says. She folds a yellow T-shirt. "This is the only thing. Everything else will be too hot."

"What did you wear last summer?" I ask.

"Nothing cute," Sam answers. She packs a pair of jeans.

I scoot part of the pile over into one big mountain and sit on the floor. I am really trying to be mature and not take my disappointment out on Sam. "Tell me about your trip to Costa Rica. What are you all going to do?"

"Well, it's going to be more work than fun," she says. "Mr. Flores has us waking up early to volunteer at a school where we'll work with children and help out the teachers. We'll have to write a reflection in Spanish at the end of every day."

I ask her, "You have to have some free time, right?"

"Well, I think we're going zip-lining or something at Manuel Antonio National Park. And I heard that we might hike through Monteverde—which doesn't sound *that* fun," Sam says. "I know it's famous for orchids or something, but I hate hiking, especially in the heat." Sam is not a good actress, but I do appreciate that she's trying to downplay this trip.

"Well, whatever you'll be doing, you'll be in Cartago, Costa Rica. Take pictures. Of everything. I want all the details when you get back."

"So, what are you going to do during spring break?"

"Well, I won't be going to Costa Rica," I say.

"Are you mad I'm going?"

"No. I'm mad I'm not going."

"Jade, this isn't fair. You get chosen to do cool things all the time, and the one time the school chooses me for something, you get jealous?" Sam throws a bunch of tank tops into her suitcase.

"Why does everyone think I get all the fun stuff?" I ask Sam. "SAT prep is not cool. Tutoring after school is not fun. You're going to Costa Rica—"

"You went to the symphony. I've never been to the symphony."

"You'd rather go to the Oregon Symphony than to Costa Rica?"

"Jade—"

"I didn't think so."

Sam opens her closet. There's a plastic shoe holder hanging from the back of the door. She pulls out a pair of flip-flops from one of the plastic sleeves and adds them to her suitcase. "Can we please talk about something else?" she says.

"Why can't we talk about this?" I ask. "Why can't we talk about how unfair it is that at St. Francis, people who look like *you* get signed up for programs that take them to Costa Rica, and people who look like me get signed up for programs that take them downtown?"

I want to get up right now, want to end the conversation and leave. But I can hear Maxine telling me to stop quitting. To work through the hard stuff. I try to get Sam to understand how I feel. "That study abroad program—the one *I* should be part of—isn't about giving a man a fish or teaching a man to fish. And there's no talk of a contaminated river, because people like *you* own the river and the fish—"

"What are you talking about? I don't own anything!" Sam's eyes well up with tears. "I don't like what you're saying, Jade. I've been nothing but a friend to you. Why can't you be happy for me? Just this once. All the times you've come to me bragging about everything you get to do with Maxine? I've always been happy for you."

"Bragging? You think I was bragging? I was just doing what friends do: sharing about my day, sharing my life with you—"

"And I want to be able to share this with you, but how can I when you're moping around and making me feel guilty? I'm sorry you're not going, Jade. I want you to be there, but I can't change that. What do you want from me?"

Before I even answer, Sam's tears are falling, like she already knows she won't be able to give me whatever it is I'm about to ask for, and so now tears are tangled in my throat. "Sometimes, Sam, I just want you to listen. Anytime I bring up feeling like I'm being treated unfairly because I'm a black girl, you downplay it or make excuses. You never admit it's about race."

"I—I don't think it always is," Sam says.

"Of course you don't," I say. "You know nothing about being nominated into programs that want to *fix* you."

Sam's face contorts into confusion. "What do you mean?"

I can't control my breath. My chest heaves and words escape between shallow gasps. "I just want to be normal. I just want a teacher to look at me and think I'm worth a trip to Costa Rica. Not just that I need *help* but that I can help someone else. You keep saying we're not that different, but have you ever wondered why you don't get the same *opportunities* I get?"

She wipes her tears.

I swallow mine.

She keeps packing.

I stand. "I should go. I want to get on the bus before it's dark."

Sam doesn't turn around, doesn't speak. She keeps packing.

I know Maxine says there are some friends who are worth fighting for, but sometimes it's just easier to walk away.

"Have fun in Costa Rica," I tell her. I don't say, *See you when you get back.*

55

miedo
fear

With a whole week off from school, there's plenty of time to hang with Lee Lee and Andrea. We are tired of going to Jantzen Beach shopping center. For one, we don't have money to buy anything, and two, Lee Lee's ex works at Target and she doesn't want to run into him.

Andrea says, "Let's walk to Columbia Park."

"You just want to see if Tyrell is there," Lee Lee says. She puts on her shoes.

"Ain't nobody thinking about Tyrell," Andrea says. "He's at work, anyway. He gets off at six o'clock."

Lee Lee nudges me, laughing. "For someone who's not thinking about him, she sure does know his schedule by heart."

Andrea gets even more irritated once I start laughing. And that just makes us laugh harder. I tell her, "You know you like him."

Lee Lee says, "And he *been* wanting to date you, Andrea. So what's the problem? Just go on and get it over with."

Andrea ignores us, acting like she can't hear a thing we're saying. She walks outside and waits on the porch until me and Lee Lee are ready.

Once we're outside, I take my camera out.

Andrea is still in her funky mood. "Jade, don't take no pictures of me without letting me know," she says.

I tell her, "Candid shots are the best kind." I snap the button before she can disagree.

"Jade!"

I check the screen to see the photo. "You look fine. Just act normal."

We keep walking. The whole way, I'm documenting the city, taking photos of strangers I've never seen, strangers I see every day. Like the woman who is always sitting on her porch, knitting something.

"Let's stop at Frank's," Lee Lee says. The three of us put our money together. Frank ends up giving us extra wings, and he stuffs the white paper bag with JoJos. I grab one of the free newspapers from the stand and put it into my bag. Inspiration for later.

We walk out of the store, eating and talking. First about Lee Lee's ex, because even though she can't bear to see him, she can't stop talking about him. When we turn the corner, just ahead of us, about a block away, we see a police car, its lights flashing.

We stop.

White cops have pulled over a black woman. We walk closer. Stop at enough distance not to be noticed but close enough to be witnesses.

I can hear Lee Lee clutch the paper bag. Andrea's chest rises and rises. I grab the string of my camera. Remind myself to use it if necessary.

Everyone seems calm. There's no commotion, but still, I start taking photos. I don't know why. I just need to. The officer writes something on a notepad and then gives the slip of paper to the woman. He goes back to his car. She drives away.

The three of us stand still.

I hear rattling, something like crumpling paper. I look to my left and see Lee Lee's hand is shaking. Her whole arm is having a fit. Her fist is clenching the bag like an anchor to keep her from falling to the ground. I tell her, "It's okay." I take her hand, but she pulls away. "It's okay, Lee Lee. Come on. Let's go."

Lee Lee looks at me like she heard me but didn't understand me.

"We're okay. It's okay," I repeat. "She's fine, she's fine."

Lee Lee walks.

Andrea walks on the other side of her, putting her in the middle of us. I pry the bag out of Lee Lee's hand. Put her hand in mine and let her squeeze it as hard as she needs to. We walk down the street. The three of us, hand in hand. "It's okay," I say. "We're fine, we're fine. Everything's okay."

56

liberar
to release

I print the photos I took today. Leave all of them intact, except the ones of the officers, their cars, those merry-go-round lights.

Every tear I've been holding in goes onto the page.

Tears for Mom's swollen ankles after a long day of work, for her jar of pennies. Tears for every "almost," for every "Things will be different next time." Tears for what happened with Mrs. Weber, the lady at the mall, the boys at Dairy Queen.

I didn't realize how much I was holding in. How many cries I've buried.

I have no more room.

So I let it all out.

Tears for every name of unarmed black men and women I know of who've been assaulted or murdered by the police are inked on the page. Their names whole and vibrant against the backdrop of black sadness.

Their names. So many, they spill off the page.

57

silencio
silence

I know Sam is back from Costa Rica. I sit on the bus, and the closer we get to her stop, the more my stomach turns. I don't know what to say to her, but I know I need to say something. The bus pulls up to her stop. A man gets on and walks all the way to the back, even though there are free seats closer to the front. A pregnant woman gets on and sits in the first available seat.

Sam is not there.

I think maybe she's so exhausted from the trip that she overslept and now is running late. I look out of the window, thinking I might see her running down the block, calling out for the bus not to leave. But she is not there.

My stomach settles. But just a little. Sooner or later we're going to have to talk.

Not having Sam's company makes the ride seem longer. When I get to school, Sam is already there, which means she took an earlier bus or her grandpa dropped her off. I see her walking down the hall toward her first-period class. Instead of running up to her and trying to start a conversation, I test out a wave to see what her response will be.

She waves back, but there is no smile. There is no stopping and waiting for me to catch up with her so we can talk. And so I know her coming to school on her own this morning was not about being too tired to get up early. It was about not wanting to be with me.

58

pieza por pieza
piece by piece

Today Maxine takes me to the Esplanade. I've never walked the whole thing, and I have a feeling Maxine is going to want to do just that, because she is dressed in sweats and Nikes. Portland's Esplanade is a path for cyclists and pedestrians, and it goes along the Willamette River. I love seeing Portland's waterfront park and bridges all at once. Camera in hand, I take photos as we walk, capturing the boats on the water.

A cyclist dings his bell, so we step aside.

We find a bench and sit down. The Tilikum Crossing bridge behind us, the Hawthorne Bridge in front of us. The sun is warm, but every few minutes Portland's breeze embraces us.

Maxine asks, "So, what's been on your mind lately?"

I tell her how I've been thinking about being stitched together and coming undone. "Do you ever feel that way?" I ask.

"Absolutely," Maxine says.

"Really?"

"When I went to St. Francis, most people assumed that because I was black, I must be on scholarship."

"I'm on scholarship," I remind her.

"I know. But you were awarded a scholarship because you are smart, not because you are black," Maxine says. "I got tired of people assuming things about me without getting to know me." Maxine squints and goes into her purse. She digs for a moment and then pulls out her sunglasses. "Sometimes, in class, if something about race came up, I was looked at to give an answer as if I could speak on behalf of all black people," Maxine says. "It was exhausting."

"Very exhausting," I say.

A couple walks to the edge of the boardwalk and takes a selfie.

I tell Maxine, "I didn't think you dealt with any of that at St. Francis. Seems like you really liked it there."

Maxine crosses her legs, leans back against the bench. "I loved a lot about St. Francis, but just because I had a good experience there doesn't mean everything was perfect," Maxine scoots closer to me, lowers her voice and says, "And to be honest, not all of the negative messages were from white people."

"What do you mean?" I ask.

"You remember my dad is in real estate, right? Well, when I was a little girl, like elementary-school age, I'd overhear him tell his clients who were black that they should take down the photos and artwork in their homes in order to have a better chance to sell."

"Really?"

"Yeah. And I never heard him say that to white families," Maxine says. "And so, I don't know. I think I internalized all of that." She stops talking for a moment, like for the first time she is realizing something. "I guess it made me feel like blackness needed to be hidden, toned down, and that whiteness was good, more acceptable," Maxine says.

Then she laughs as a memory comes to her mind. "I remember being so embarrassed about having friends over to my house."

"Are you serious? Why? You have a nice house; it's like a mansion."

"Well, it's, you know—*black*."

We laugh. Hard.

"I mean, the art on the walls, the food my family eats," Maxine explains. "When I was in high school, I wasn't sure how my white friends would react. Remember—I grew up with parents who believed you should tone down your blackness when in public. I didn't know how to function when the public came to my private home. I grew up feeling tremendous pride in our culture, what we as a people overcame and accomplished, but at the same time there was this message from my parents telling me not to be *too* black. At school, with my white friends and teachers, there were all these stereotypes I felt I had to dispel, and, with a lot of my black friends, I had to prove that I was black enough—whatever that means. It was complicated," Maxine says.

All this time I've been thinking how easy Maxine has it. How she has no idea how I feel, what I go through. We start walking again, making our way back to the car. The boardwalk is crowded now, cyclists and joggers whizzing by. Every now and then we see two women speed-walking and pushing strollers. Makes me wonder if they planned to get pregnant at the same time so they could have their children together. Makes me wonder if I will ever have a child and if Lee Lee will ever have a child and if we'll ever push strollers and walk along a boardwalk together.

Clouds are moving in. Maxine lifts her sunglasses up and nestles them into her hair. I ask Maxine, "What are you thinking about?"

She smiles and says, "My grandmother. I'm thinking about how she'd say that sometimes, it's just good to talk it out, you know?"

"Yeah."

"My grandmother called it bearing witness. She'd sit on the porch with her sister and talk the night away. Sometimes gossiping, sometimes praying. I'd hear them confide in each other, telling each other things I knew I wasn't supposed to know anything about." Maxine hits the button on her keychain to unlock her door. We get in. "I didn't get it as a kid. I mean, nothing got resolved, necessarily, so I thought it was silly to just sit and rehash everything that was wrong with the world," Maxine says.

"Yeah, that's kind of depressing," I say.

"But I think what my grandmother was saying is that it feels good to know someone knows your story, that someone took you in," Maxine says. "She'd tell me, it's how we heal."

59

escuchar
to listen

The next time I see Maxine, it's for Woman to Woman's very first Money Matters workshop. We're having the meeting at a small church not too far away from my house. The pastor is letting us use the space. I love that I didn't even need to take a bus or get a ride from Maxine to get here. I love that once it gets started, Sabrina says, "I'd like to give a big thank-you to Jade, who is the one who suggested today's workshop topic. So if you like today's session, you owe it to her."

Jasmine starts clapping, and then everyone joins in.

Sabrina pauses, letting the applause fill the space. "I want you all to know that your feedback is welcomed here. This is your program, and we want you to get the most out of it."

Sabrina introduces our guests for the day. The first person is

Maxine's friend Bailey, which is a surprise to me. Maxine leans in and whispers to me, "I couldn't let you in on everything."

Sabrina tells us, "Bailey is going to focus on how to make and manage your money in college." Then she says, "Aka don't get any credit cards!"

The panelists laugh, and our mentors all respond with a chorus of agreement.

Sabrina introduces the rest of the panelists and tells us, "This is the first of many conversations, so if your question doesn't get answered today, don't worry."

By the end of the panel, my fingers are cramping because I've been taking notes nonstop. There are handouts, but I didn't want to write on them. I want to save them and share them with Mom and E.J. and Lee Lee.

Bring back something other than food this time.

60

anticiparse

to anticipate

I post my schedule on the fridge for Mom. I've put a big circle around the third Saturday of the month because that's when Woman to Woman is going to visit Maxine's sister's gallery. Sabrina was not playing around when she said she took our input seriously. Mia is going to talk to us about being an entrepreneur, and then we'll get a tour of her gallery. She's closing to the public that day, and it'll be just us.

Mom teases me, "You can hardly wait, huh? Bet you are counting down the days."

"No, I'm not," I tell her.

But Mom knows me better than anyone could ever know me.

Three more weeks.

Twenty-one days.

Five hundred and four hours.

61

las manos
hands

E.J. has a gig deejaying for a new restaurant. He works every Thursday and Friday night now, so usually it's only me at home. Maxine calls and asks what I'm up to. I tell her, "Nothing, about to take out my braids so my mom can redo my hair."

"Want some company? Four hands are better than two," she says. "I can help you take them out."

I call my mom, ask if it's okay for Maxine to come over. She doesn't mind.

I tell Maxine to come over because I could really use the help. These braids are small, and I don't feel like being up all night, doing my hair. As soon as I hang up the phone, I realize I just agreed to let Maxine come over and stay awhile. I am used to her stopping by for only a moment to pick me up, maybe look at my new art projects. But to stay, for hours at a time? I get anxious about the things she'll see that maybe she hasn't noticed before, like how the dining room table isn't a real dining room table and how none of the furniture matches, or how there's a crack in the ceiling, chipped paint on some of the walls.

When Maxine gets to my house, I get a brown paper bag, open it, and set it on the floor next to the sofa. I go to the bathroom and return with two small combs, a pair of scissors, and a small squirt bottle full of water. "Ready?" I ask.

"Yep." Maxine grabs a throw pillow from the sofa and gives it to me. She sits on the sofa. I sit on the floor, propped up by the pillow between her legs.

Maxine holds a handful of braids and clips the ends with the scissors. We start unbraiding, throwing the used added hair into the bag. After my hair is unbraided, Maxine sprays my hair with water to make it easier to comb through. The mist tickles the back of my neck. She parts my hair into fours, gathers the bottom section in her palm, and pulls the comb through my hair. It feels so good to get my hair combed. To feel the teeth raking gently against my scalp.

I tie my hair up and clean up the living room. Maxine is just about to leave when Mom's key opens the door. "Hi, Maxine," Mom says. "Hey, Jade." She kisses me on my cheek. Then she looks at my scarf. "You still want me to braid your hair tomorrow? We better get started on taking that down. It's getting late."

I take my scarf off. "Maxine helped me."

Mom looks at me. "Well, let me comb it out for you—"

"She did," I tell her.

"Oh," Mom says. "Well, that was nice of you, Maxine." Mom's face is smiling, but her voice is not.

"No problem at all," Maxine says.

Mom walks into the kitchen. "Well, since you don't need me to do your hair, guess I'll get dinner started. Unless Maxine already fed you."

"I haven't eaten yet," I say.

"I better go so you all can have dinner," Maxine says.

Mom comes back to the living room. "You don't have to leave, Maxine. Stay for dinner."

"Oh, no. You two haven't seen each other all day—"

"I insist," Mom says.

"Okay, well, thanks." Maxine sits back down.

Mom calls out from the kitchen, "One of these days, I'm going to try some of the recipes you gave Jade."

"You'll have to tell me how that goes," Maxine says. "I'm still experimenting and learning."

"Learning what? How to cook?" Mom peeks back into the living room.

"I'm good with salads," Maxine says. "But, ah, everything else? Nah."

Mom laughs. She waves Maxine into the kitchen. "Come on in here and let me show you a thing or two," she says.

Mom and Maxine start cooking. I ask if I can help, but Mom says I need to finish my homework. So I sit at the table in the kitchen and practice new vocabulary, purposely saying out loud the words that pertain to cooking.

To Peel—Pelar
To Cut—Cortar
To Chop—Picar
To Add—Agregar, incorporar
To Mix—Mezclar
To Combine—Combinar

The aroma from Mom's chopped herbs and sprinkled spices swims through the house. The pots are shaking to a boil; the oven is warming. I get Mom to try a few words. And while I am teaching Mom, she is teaching Maxine what a pinch of that and a dab of this means. While we wait for the food to cook, Mom adds in lessons on love and tells Maxine the remedy to a broken heart. Tells her how to move on. Mom looks at me, says, "You paying attention? You'll need this one day."

62

practicar
to practice

It's the third Saturday of the month.

Maxine and I are on our way to Mia's gallery. The radio is on, and we are singing along as loud as we can. When it goes off, Maxine asks, "What do you know about that song? That was out when I was in middle school."

I laugh.

Too many commercials come on, so Maxine changes the station.

We get to the gallery just in time for Sabrina's introduction. "I am so honored to be in this space today and so very excited for you all to meet the woman who owns this art gallery," she says. "I hope you enjoy this conversation with our host, Mia, one of the few black entrepreneurs on Jackson Avenue. Her gallery opened last year, and we are very fortunate she is giving us her time today."

We all cheer and applaud as Sabrina welcomes Mia to the front of the room. Mia speaks about her journey to becoming a business owner. Then she shows us slides of her art gallery when it was just an abandoned building, and all the ways it's transformed into what it is today. "I like to think of this gallery as the people's gallery. That means, I curate work that speaks to current issues, that is made by artists from marginalized groups, and I also make it a point not to showcase only well-known artists who you all may learn about in school. I want to introduce audiences to contemporary artists, young artists. Black and Latino artists. And so this exhibit is in line with that." Mia points to the walls.

I look around the gallery, and I can't wait to get up close, really study the work. We are surrounded by life-size portraits of black women. They look like if you walk up to the paintings and say hello, they will say hi back to you. They look like regal queens but also like my next-door neighbors. Mia says, "This collection is Kehinde Wiley's first series dedicated to African American women. He's a contemporary artist, and in this work he used women from the streets of New York City as inspiration and based the poses off historical portraits by painters like Jacques-Louis David and other painters who almost exclusively painted white women. So this is an exciting day for me, to be able to share this work—a work celebrating black women and giving them a place in art history—with you all, young black girls who I hope find your place in this world one day," Mia says. "Any questions?"

A few people ask questions, and then Mia releases us to roam around the space. Sabrina calls out, reminding us to think about what we're feeling and experiencing as we take in the images, because we will close the day with a reflection.

I look at the collection up close, taking my time to notice every detail. My favorite portrait is of a woman who is thick like me, and dark brown like coffee beans. I can't wait to bring Lee Lee here. And Mom.

Maxine stands next me.

I tell her, "I think this might be the best outing we've had."

"Well, I'm glad to hear that," she says. "I wasn't sure you were enjoying yourself. You didn't ask any questions."

"Oh, that's because I wasn't sure if my question was appropriate to ask right now," I tell her.

Maxine laughs. "What could you possibly want to know?" Her eyebrows are arched with suspicion.

"Nothing bad—I just wanted to know if Mia offers internships. I'd love to work here and learn more about the business of running an art gallery."

"Oh! You could have totally asked that," she says. "Just go over to her and let her know you're interested."

"I can't do that," I tell her.

"Yes, you can," Maxine says.

I can. I can speak for myself.

I walk over to Mia, and as I approach her, she smiles. "Hey, Jade, so good to see you again."

"Good to see you too," I say. "I love this exhibit."

"I'm so glad." Mia is standing there, normal and casual, with no idea that my heart is pounding on the inside.

"I, um, I really like what you said about why you started your business," I tell her. "I'd like to learn more. You know, I'm an artist—"

"Yes, Maxine keeps telling me that. I'd love to see some of your work."

"Maybe I can come by one day and bring a few pieces." I can see Sabrina gathering everyone to close the day. I am running out of time to ask about the internship. Mia says I can stop by anytime, so then I say, "Maybe I'll come by next week after school. I'd like to talk with you about the possibility of interning here. Do you have internships?"

"I do," Mia tells me. "I have two paid internship positions. I'd love for you to work here. Let's talk more about it. In the meantime, I'll get you an application so we can get the process started." Mia walks to the back and goes into her office. She returns, the application in her hand.

Sabrina calls out, "Okay, everybody! We're going to end the day with a closing reflection. I want you all to close your eyes, think about our time together, everything you saw, the information you learned. Now think of one word you're feeling, and once everyone has their words, we'll go around and put those words into the space."

The room is silent.

I don't need to think hard. My word comes immediately.

Inspired.

63

soledad
loneliness

How I Know Sam's Not My Friend Anymore:

No more bus rides to and from school together.

When Mr. Flores tells us to choose a partner, she doesn't choose me.

Even when something is funny, she doesn't turn to me and laugh. She'd rather hold it in, keep her joy to herself.

64

oportunidad
opportunity

Woman to Woman's second Money Matters workshop has ended, and the guest speaker is bombarded by all the mentees rushing to meet him. Sabrina calls me over to the back of the church, telling me she has something to ask me. "As you know, we're having our annual fundraiser soon, and I wanted to know if you'd contribute a piece of art for our auction."

"Me?"

"Yes, you. We'd love to showcase some student work this year," Sabrina says. "You can donate something you already have, or if you want, you can make something new."

Of course I tell her yes.

Maxine and I talk about it the whole way home. She parked her car at my house before the workshop and we walked over together.

When we get to my house, Maxine comes in to say hello to Mom. I tell Mom about the auction, and the first thing she says is, "So they're going to make money off your art? What do you get out of it?"

I tell her what Sabrina told me. "I get exposure. There are going to be a lot of people there—people with money— and you never know what could happen. Plus, it helps raise money for us to go on all those outings and, of course, it'll help the scholarship fund. I like being able to say I'm not just getting an opportunity from Woman to Woman, but that I am helping to keep it thriving. Don't you think that's a good thing?"

"I do," Mom says. "I just want to make sure you're okay with it. That it's really something you want to do." Then she looks at Maxine and says, "What do you think? You think it's all right for her to do this? Aren't these kind of events fancy and full of rich white folks? I don't want people gawking over her. I mean, I know she's all excited about it, but I don't want her to come home, feeling like she's been a zoo animal all night. You know what I mean?"

Maxine nods. "I absolutely know what you mean. I've had to participate in my fair share of fundraisers and gala events. I can give her some tips on what to expect," Maxine says. "And I'll be there looking out for her," she promises.

"Well, good. Glad she won't be there by herself," Mom says.

"And you know, it will be good for Jade to speak about her work and meet and greet people who are interested in supporting young women. They need to meet her," Maxine explains.

"Well," Mom says. "I guess they do." She smiles so big, bigger than any smile I've seen on her face in a long while. "Our little artist is doing big things, huh, Maxine?"

I like that she said *our*, like she's okay with sharing me.

Mom goes to the kitchen. "Maxine, you been using any of those skills I taught you?"

"Well, you see, what happened was—"

"No excuses," Mom says, laughing and shaking her head.

Maxine and I go to the kitchen too.

Mom is cutting up a rotisserie chicken. There's a bag of kale sitting on a cutting board and a box of croutons on the countertop. "Thought I'd try one of those healthy-living recipes," she says. Mom asks Maxine to rinse the kale.

I take out bowls and forks. I set them on the table and ask Maxine, "So, what is it going to be like?"

She tells me it's a cocktail party. "But of course, *you* won't be drinking." She laughs.

"I know that's right," Mom says.

Maxine tells us, "This year the fundraiser will be at Mia's gallery. There will be a live jazz band, and people will mingle and talk and buy art. And toward the end, Sabrina will say a few words about the program. That's all."

"So, I don't have to make a speech or anything, right?"

"No," Maxine says, "but since your art is being featured as the student art, I'm sure folks will want to talk with you. You should think of how you want to represent yourself. Come up with a few things you want to say about your art, about the program, about your goals in life." She tells me, "You'll be fine. Just be yourself."

65

confianza
confidence

I am the most dressed up I've ever been. Other than these heels
Maxine suggested I buy, I am feeling good. By the end of the
night, though, I think I might be limping back home. Maxine
helped me pick out makeup. At first I didn't want to wear any,
but now that she's finished painting my face, I have to admit, I
really like it.

"Okay, my turn," Maxine says.

I leave my room and let her have some privacy to get ready.
As I wait in the living room, E.J. comes home. "You got a date
or something?" he asks.

"No, E.J. I'm going to a Woman to Woman event," I say.

"Oh, all right, then. I know I've been missing in action a little
bit, but you better not be dating nobody without my knowing."

I roll my eyes.

"You think I'm playing?"

Maxine comes out of my bedroom, all transformed out of her jeans and T-shirt. E.J. looks her up and down. "You sure you not going out on a double date?"

Maxine laughs. "What kind of mentor would I be?" she asks.

"Just checking. I mean, you two are looking real nice," E.J. says.

"Thanks, E.J.," I say. "But I think it's ridiculous that you think I could only be getting dressed up for a guy."

"Well, you look beautiful, whoever it's for."

I think for a moment and then tell him, "It's for me."

Once we get to the fundraiser, I don't feel as out of place as I thought I would. That prep time with Maxine paid off. She was right about it all, except she forgot the part about how good the food would be, how waiters walk around bringing you tray after tray of huge shrimp, stuffed mushrooms. Maxine didn't tell me how I'd feel like some kind of celebrity, the way everyone keeps coming up to me, asking, "Are you the young lady who made that art piece? It's lovely." They swarm around my framed art, hovering at the wall like bees, making bids for the silent auction and walking away, then coming back again to see if anyone else has made a bid.

I can't believe people are going back and forth about who wants to buy something I made.

There's so much happening all at once. Music from the jazz ensemble playing in the background, servers coming up to me every few seconds with a new offering. I am standing with Maxine and a woman named Gina, who is one of the board members of Woman to Woman.

"I love your work," Gina says to me. She is a short white woman with black hair. We talk for a while about art because she used to paint when she was younger. "I don't do it as much as I'd like to, but I pull out my brushes every now and then," she tells me. Gina gives me her card. "I'd love to talk with you more about your future plans for college. Keep in touch."

Another couple walks up to us. They are holding hands, and everything about them looks expensive. Even the smiles on their faces. They give me compliments and ask me what school I go to, what colleges I am interested in, what I like about Woman to Woman.

I answer their questions and tell them, "The thing I like most about this program is that the mentors and program director really listen." They are all looking at me and smiling and drinking their wine and then smiling some more. I get what Mom meant by feeling like I'm on display. But Maxine was right too; if I'm going to be on display, I might as well use the opportunity to say something worthwhile, so when the man with the perfect smile asks, "And what have you learned?" I tell him I've learned I don't have to wait to be given an opportunity, but that I can make an opportunity and use my voice to speak up for what I need and want.

The man with the perfect smile says, "My, I am so impressed. You are so articulate, so well spoken, and—"

Before he can finish his sentence, Gina cuts him off. "What did you expect?" she asks. She says this with a forced grin on her face, a tone in her voice that is trying to hide its irritation. She stands closer to me, almost shielding me from him. "Woman to Woman is full of talented, smart, passionate young women from all over the city."

The man's face tenses up, and I don't know what to do. Thankfully, Maxine is standing next to me. She steps forward a bit and says, "Yes, and I'm so lucky to work with them."

Just then one of the servers comes up to us. "Stuffed mushroom, anyone?"

We each take one, and there's barely time for the awkwardness to settle in, because Sabrina takes the mic and makes a short speech.

At the end of the night, the winner of the auction comes up to me, smiling, my piece in his hands. He is a tall brown man with a watch on his wrist that says he could buy all of the art at this auction and not miss a dime. "My name is Andrew, and I'm very glad to be the new owner of this piece of art. I hear you are the artist."

I shake his hand. Firm, like Maxine taught me. "My name is Jade."

"I've got my eye on you," he says. "I hope to see more work from you in the future. Do you have more pieces like this?"

"Oh, no," I tell him. "I created this especially for this event." Maxine clears her throat, giving me a glance nudging me to say more. "Right now I am working on a series of collages about police brutality against unarmed black women and men." I also tell him all about my pieces on York and Lewis and Clark, and my vision to make beauty out of everyday things, to find beauty in the disregarded.

Andrew says, "The world is in for a big awakening once you really get your work out there." He reaches into his pocket and pulls out a business card. "If there's any way I can help you, shoot me an e-mail."

Throughout the night, guests keep coming up to me and congratulating me and handing me their business cards. Maxine smiles at me. "Hold on to those cards you're getting. Follow up tomorrow."

"Okay." I slide them into my purse, which is only big enough for my lip gloss, mints, house key, and these cards.

Sabrina motions for Maxine to come over and talk with one of the board members. I stay behind, looking at the space on the wall where my art was. I think about these people who don't even know me but want to support me, and I am feeling seen and heard.

66

la tarea
homework

The next day, Lee Lee comes over after school so we can do our homework together. Hers is more interesting than mine. She is writing an essay about how media is used in social movements.

"I'm comparing how in 1955 the civil rights movement got a lot of attention because *Jet* magazine printed the photo of Emmett Till. Our teacher told us that decision put a face to racism in the South. People all over the world reacted. So, yeah, we have to write about that and connect it to how Facebook and Twitter are being used by activists now."

"Your teacher assigned this?"

"Yeah. I wrote the first draft, but now she's saying I need to revise it." Lee Lee sounds so annoyed by that, but I'd rather do her homework than mine. I don't think any of the teachers at St. Francis would assign that.

When we're finished with our homework, Lee Lee says, "You want to hear my poem for Natasha Ramsey? I'm still working on it, but I think it's almost finished."

I listen to Lee Lee read her poem, and I want to say something more profound, but all I can think of is, "Wow, Lee Lee, that's really good."

"Thanks," Lee Lee says. She sets her notebook down and looks over the poem again. "I want to do something with this."

"Like what?" I ask.

"I don't know. Everyone's poems in class were so good. Seems like a waste to just write them and no one hears them except us."

When Lee Lee says this, I think about Mia's gallery. "I have an idea," I say.

For the rest of the night we think up a plan to have an open mic and art show in honor of Natasha Ramsey. We get so caught up with our idea that we plan every detail. Lee Lee will be the MC. She'll open and close the event with two of her poems. We'll ask students from her school to come and share their poems too. I'll have some of my art on display, and hopefully we can get some other visual artists from local schools. I'll ask Josiah if he'll be our social media person and help us promote it.

Lee Lee says, "Should we charge people to get in and give the proceeds to Natasha's family? I heard there's some kind of fund where people can donate to help with the cost of medical bills."

I think about the benefit gala and all those people coming up to me, giving me their cards, saying, "Call me if you need anything," and "Keep in touch." I tell Lee Lee, "I don't want any excuse for people not to come, so let's not charge. But we can sell the art. I know some people who will buy art for a good cause."

We are all ready to choose a date when we realize we haven't even asked Mia if she'll host the event. I sure hope she meant it when she said her gallery was for the people.

67

renacimiento
rebirth

I've been combining moments from different photos, blending decades, people, and worlds that don't belong together. Knitting history into the beautiful, bloody tapestry it is.

Emmett Till meets Trayvon Martin and Michael Brown.

Rosa Parks and Sandra Bland talk with each other under southern trees.

Coretta Scott King is holding Aiyana Mo'Nay Stanley-Jones in her arms.

The faces lie on top of newspaper articles and headlines, only I take the words from the headlines and spell out new titles, rewrite history. Make it so all these people are living and loving and being.

68

legado
legacy

1805.

Lewis and Clark and the rest of the explorers reached the Pacific Ocean in November. They established Fort Clatsop, near Astoria, Oregon, and stayed there for the winter. On March 23, 1806, they headed to St. Louis. The eight-thousand-mile journey had ended.

After all those days searching for the Missouri River, after being trusted to carry a gun, after being listened to, after having some kind of say, York returned to St. Louis with the others.

The others were welcomed back as national heroes.

They were given 320 acres of land and double pay.

But York? He didn't get anything.

And maybe he was okay with that. Maybe he knew getting land and money was out of the question. But could he keep his freedom? Could he continue to walk the earth, going where he pleased, having a say, being part of a community? When he asked for his freedom, Clark said no. Clark said, "Who does this slave think he is?"

All York wanted was to be close to his wife, who lived in Kentucky. All York wanted was to hold on to that feeling, that feeling when you stand at the ocean, letting the water rush up to your feet and run away again. That feeling of looking out and not being able to see an end or beginning. That feeling that reminds you how massive this world is, how tiny but powerful humans are.

1816.

Clark eventually gave York his freedom.

I wonder what it would have been like if York had received that land and that money, and his freedom. What would he have built? Would he have left it to his children? Would they have done something with it and passed it on, and then their children's children would have passed it on? And isn't this what the man in the Money Matters workshop was telling us when he was explaining how it is that some are rich and some are poor?

Isn't that how it works? You pass on what you were given.

But York, what could he give?

69

trabajar
to work

Mia was so excited about our idea that she decided to call up a few of her friends, and now we have three professional artists who've donated their work for the event. We also put a call out to local high schools for students who want to submit work. Mia is in charge of all that, thank goodness. All I have to focus on is making my piece. I thought since Lee Lee has a poem written for the occasion, I should take inspiration from her poem. We've been in the kitchen all day, working. Lee Lee is revising her poem one last time, and I am working on the images.

The only noise in the kitchen is her pen on the page crossing out and adding in, writing and rewriting stanzas, mixed with the slicing of scissors, the tearing of paper. On and on we go until the sun meets moon.

70

arreglar
to fix

Mr. Flores tells the class we will be working in pairs today. He puts me and Sam together. "These are your conversations for the activity," he says. The words on the cards are written in English. It's up to us to say them in Spanish. The answer key is on the back of the card. He gives each pair three cards with different conversations on them. "It doesn't matter if these are or are not your real answers," Mr. Flores says. "The point is to practice having conversations."

Sam bites her lip and picks up the card that's on top.

Sam: "Jade, ¿qué vas a hacer esta noche?"
Me: "Voy a ir a bailar. ¿Quieres venir?"
Sam: "¡Me encantaría!"

Me: "A las diez."
Sam: "¡Buenísimo!"

And then we switch roles. But instead of saying what's on the card, I talk to her in my own words.

Me: "Lo siento."
Sam: "Yo también."
Me: "Maxine has been on me about quitting things. She says I can't just give up so easily. Especially on people."
Sam: "My grandpa says I have a lot to learn. He says I need to listen more."

Sam puts the cards down on the table. "He's been giving me a ride to school. That's why I haven't been on the bus."
Me: "I figured."
Sam's shoulders settle into her body, and she sits back in the chair. I am fine to leave it at that. This is a good start. Maybe we can talk more after school, but then Sam says, real low, "Sometimes, I don't know—I'm just uncomfortable talking about this stuff. And I don't know what to say to you when something's happened to you that's not fair. Like that day at the mall. I felt horrible, but what was I supposed to do?"

"Sometimes, it isn't about you doing anything. When you brush it off like I'm making it up or blowing things out of proportion, it makes me feel like my feelings don't matter to you."

Mr. Flores calls out to us that it's time to go on to the next activity. He walks past our desks to collect the cards. He looks at us, like he knows we weren't doing the assignment. Like he knows we really needed to talk about something else.

71

redimir
to redeem

At the end of Spanish class Mr. Flores asks if I can stay and talk with him. He makes small talk with me while everyone gathers their things and leaves the classroom. "Well, I have to say, I'm very proud of you for what you're doing for Natasha Ramsey," Mr. Flores says. "I'll be there for sure. And I'm giving extra credit to students who go. I'll announce that tomorrow," he tells me. "The art department is also encouraging students to go."

"Thanks."

Mr. Flores closes the door once everyone is out of the room. "I wanted to talk to you about the study abroad program," he says. "I've really been thinking about what you said. And I wanted to let you know I am so sorry I overlooked you."

It feels strange hearing these words from a teacher.

"I wanted to let you know I spoke with Mrs. Parker and shared your concerns. I told her I agreed with you. I also asked if I could secure you a spot for next year, and she said yes."

"Wait. Really? She said yes?" I want him to repeat it. Just to make sure I heard him right.

"Really," Mr. Flores says. "And so, as long as you continue to meet the requirements, you have a guaranteed spot for next spring."

"Thank you, Mr. Flores. Thank you."

"Don't thank me. You did this."

72

perdón
forgiveness

How I Know Sam Is My Friend

We ride the bus to and from school together.

When Mr. Flores tells us to choose a partner, he says we can't be partners because we're together all the time.

When something is funny, we laugh loud and long even if that means we're the only ones laughing.

When something is sad, we don't hide our tears from each other.

When we misunderstand each other, we listen again. And again.

73

microfono abierto
open mic

Mom comes home. She sees me sitting with Lee Lee and Sam at the table. Her smile can barely be contained on her face. I look at her, begging her to leave, not to embarrass me. She disappears into her room.

The three of us keep planning.

E.J. is going to deejay at the event while people file in and in between each performance. Mia is in charge of any donations made or art purchased. Maxine said she'd help out with that. Mia and Maxine also took over promotion for the event, and all of us have been passing out flyers at Northside and St. Francis. We took flyers to the Native American Youth and Family Center, too. Josiah agreed to set up a live stream of the open mic for people who can't come. He has a few people from St. Francis coming to live tweet during the show. Sam is our greeter. She'll make sure guests have programs and direct them to the art exhibit.

"Are we forgetting anything?" I ask.

"What about people who aren't performing a poem or show-casing their art?" Sam asks. "I know that being in the audience is participating, but I don't know. Maybe we can think of something for people like me to do."

"What if we have poems printed out that people can read if they want?" I ask.

Lee Lee pulls out a folder from her book bag. "Yeah, people can choose from any of these. Mrs. Baker has been giving us poems as examples to use when we write our own." She flips through the handouts and pulls out a few. "These are some of my favorites," she says. She hands a stack to Sam.

Sam looks them over. "I'd love to read one of these," she says. She reads through each poem as Lee Lee cleans off the table and I make lunch. When I set the sandwiches on the table, I ask Sam if she found one. She says, "I think so," and holds up a poem by Martín Espada. "It's called 'How We Could Have Lived or Died This Way,'" she says.

"I love that one," Lee Lee says.

I ask to see the poem and then read it to myself. "Yeah, this is perfect."

74

la gente
the people

The gallery is full of family, friends, and community members. Everyone from Woman to Woman is here because Sabrina made this an official monthly outing. I try to get Jasmine and Mercedes to sign up for the open mic, but they are acting shy. Mr. Flores says he'll read and so does Hannah, who I am surprised to see here. We haven't talked since that day in the cafeteria. Bailey and Kira choose a poem to read together. And Maxine convinces Gina to do the same. They stand on the side, practicing before the show starts.

I don't realize how many people are actually here until I stand at the front of the room, which we've designated as the stage. From here, I see Dad and Mom, their eyes beaming with pride. I see Andrew, who brought some of his colleagues. Mrs. Parker is here too, with her daughter and son-in-law.

And then Lee Lee grabs my hand and says, "Look." With her eyes she points to the door. Mr. and Mrs. Ramsey are here. "We can start now," she says.

"Wait a minute." I get my camera and take a photo of the crowd. This one, I will not rip or reconfigure. This one, I will leave whole.

75

Black Girls Rising
by Lee Lee Simmons

Our black bodies, sacred.
Our black bodies, holy.

Our bodies, our own.
Every smile a protest.
Each laugh a miracle.

Piece by piece we stitch ourselves back together.
This black girl tapestry, this black body
that gets dragged out of school desk, slammed onto linoleum floor,
tossed about at pool side, pulled over and pushed onto grass,

arrested never to return home,
shot on doorsteps, on sofas while sleeping
and dreaming of our next day.

Our bodies a quilt that tells stories of the middle passage,
of roots yanked and replanted.

Our bodies a mosaic of languages forgotten,
of freedom songs and moaned prayers.

Our bodies no longer
disregarded, objectified, scrutinized.

Our bodies, our own.
Every smile a protest.
Each laugh a miracle.

Our bodies rising.
Our feet marching, legs dancing, our bellies birthing, hands
  raising,
our hearts healing, voices speaking up.

Our bodies so black, so beautiful.
Here, still.

Rising.
Rising.

76

libertad
freedom

In 1832 Clark reported that York was on his way back to St. Louis to be reunited with him. Clark said that once York was free, he didn't enjoy his freedom, and wanted to come back and work for Clark. Clark said York died of cholera along the way.

But not everyone believes that story.

Many believe that after York obtained his freedom, he traveled west again. A fur trader in north-central Wyoming said he saw a negro man who told him that the first time he came to that part of the country, he was with men named Lewis and Clark.

I see York traveling west again, knowing which way to go this time. I see him crossing rivers, crossing mountains, seeing the

Native Americans who were so awed by him. This time he is no one's servant or slave. This time he tells them the whole story, tells how he is the first of his kind.

This time he speaks for himself.

Of the art I've been making lately, this is the only one where I've included myself. I am with York, both of us with maps in our hands. Both of us black and traveling. Black and exploring. Both of us discovering what we are really capable of.

Acknowledgments

"She is a friend of my mind. She gather me, man. The pieces I am, she gather them and give them back to me in all the right order. It's good, you know, when you got a woman who is a friend of your mind."
—*Toni Morrison*, Beloved

Thank you to my mother, Carrie Watson, and my sisters, Cheryl, Trisa, and Dyan, for being my first up-close-and-personal mentors. What strong and brilliant women you are. We didn't have much growing up, but we had each other and that was enough. What a gift to have sisters who are also my friends.

To my Oregon sister-friends: Chanesa Hart and Jonena Lindsey, your love is my buoy. So many times you have kept me from drowning. Thank you. Velynn Brown and Shalanda Sims, thank you for self-made writing retreats and for dreaming big with me.

Jennifer Baker, Tracey Baptiste, Tokumbo Bodunde, Dhonielle Clayton, Nanya-Akuki Goodrich, Cydney Gray, Lisa Green, Rajeeyah Finnie-Myers, Ellen Hagan, Kamilah Aisha Moon, Robin Patterson, Olugbemisola Rhuday, Kendolyn Walker, and Ibi Zoboi, you are my home away from home. You each came into my life at the perfect time. I am forever grateful to lean on, learn from, and be loved by all of you.

I feel so blessed to have been nurtured and raised by "the village." Thank you to mentors past and present, especially Katina Collins, Crystal Jackson, and April Murchinson, who deeply impacted my high school years.

And to "I Have A Dream" Foundation, Self Enhancement, Community-Word Project, and DreamYard: working with your organizations deepened my understanding of what it means to teach for social justice, what it means to really see a young person and to come into a community with a listening heart. Every mistake, misunderstanding, challenge, and success has shaped my teaching practice and made me the educator I am today. Without your organizations, I would not have met Desiree, Ivory, Serenity, Brookielle, Domonique, Ebony, Kapri, Kia, or Sommer. I would not have witnessed Haydil, Denisse, Destiny, and Lydia setting the stage on fire with their poems. I am forever changed because of my work with these young women.

Jennifer Baker, Linda Christensen, Kori Johnson, and Meg Medina, thank you for reading early drafts and for encouraging me to tell this story. And thank you to my editor, Sarah Shumway, and the Bloomsbury team as well as my agent, Rosemary Stimola, for your continued guidance and support.